Stories to Stay Alive To

Oska von Ruhland

©2019 Oska von Ruhland
All rights reserved.

Via Amazon Kindle Direct Publishing.

OskaWrites.wordpress.com

To my readers...
Despite all things, we are still here.

Where We Can

Erode

Until We Meet Again

Bernard's Barbers

The Mane Thing

Things That Might Go Bump in the Night

The Far Away

The Grove of the Ancient Sage

Sticks and Stones

A Long Time Ahead

Despite My Own

Companion

Fishbowl

Where We Can

The streak of light began to fade into the night sky. Stars winked overhead while Asher and Karmi picked their way through the shattered undergrowth of the local woods, careful of the things they couldn't see in the dark. Asher's cane tapped against fallen branches and cracked rocks as her girlfriend helped her avoid the worst of it. Everything had been bent and knocked down by the impact. The earth beneath their feet felt unsteady and shaken, like a pan filtering

gold. Karmi took a step forward and tripped, an unseen tree trunk rolling under her foot in the shapeless darkness. She landed in the leaves of another fallen tree with a loud crunch.

"Ow! Oof, my ass. Don't come this way, it's not safe." She counted her blessings that only the branches had broken.

"Yeah, I heard that. It sounded bad. Are you okay, babe?" Asher craned her neck to squint over at the other girl.

"Yeah, I'm good. Just scratched." Karmi awkwardly straightened up and brushed herself off. "Don't worry, I'll find a clear path."

"Not if you're just going to get hurt while you're doing it. I'll be fine."

Karmi made an over-exasperated sound and grinned back at the silhouette of her girlfriend. "We're looking for a fallen star in the dark, obviously I'm going to end up a bit beat up while we're out here."

"No, that's your own choice." She carefully inched her way around the fallen tree, poking the ground experimentally with her cane until she found a few branches low-lying enough to step over. Karmi kept a strained eye on her until they were side-by-side again.

"Okay, I guess that made more sense than just going straight in." She huffed out a breath.

"Waiting for you would take all night, and we don't have that time." Asher reached out for Karmi's face, confirming where her lips were before leaning in to kiss her quickly. "Let's keep going."

Karmi grinned and followed after the other girl. Together they edged through the battered trees and broken ground until the path began to clear before them. The grass had become flattened or torn up entirely, any higher grown completely burned and destroyed. It opened out into burned earth and a large crater.

"Careful," Asher whispered, poking the charred still-hot ground. Black ash stuck to the end of her cane.

"It's warm, but it should be fine." Karmi inched her way carefully towards the edge of the crater, one hand reached back to hold onto her girlfriend. Half to help guide her in the weird dim light, and half to stop herself falling down.

They both crouched at the edge to look in, hands gripped tight together at the sight. Karmi heard Asher gasp in the deathly silence.

Beneath them, huddled into the earth from the force of its impact, lay something huge and smooth. It's body was dark and shining like polished rock. Smoke or steam rose from its surface in curls and whisps. The air stank of burned forest, bitter and dusty, with the strange chemical tang of electricity.

"I always thought meteors were more... Rocky," Karmi commented after a long silent pause.

"Maybe it's not a meteor," Asher whispered, eyes wide and sparkling.

"What do you mean? It fell outta the sky."

"Yeah, but it looks strange. What if it's, you know, extra-terrestrial?" Her voice lifted, light and excited at the last words.

"Like a UFO?" Karmi's eyes widened.

"I mean, as long as you don't know what it is and it flies, anything can be a UFO. But this doesn't count because it landed - or crashed. But it could be alien, I really think it could."

"I'm gonna touch it." Karmi crawled over the edge and skidded down the crater, kicking up chunks of ashy black earth.

"Hey! That's not fair! I can't move as fast as you," Asher called after her. She inched to the edge and slowly, carefully, made her way down the curved side.

Karmi stopped and reached for her, and together they both safely reached the bottom of the crater where the great smooth lump lay. Its surface had cooled and revealed to have a strange oil-spill like colouring. As they both reached out to touch it, it seemed to gently tremble beneath their fingers, smooth body roughed by its hard landing.

The area beneath their fingers lit up as their skin made contact and they backed up quickly. But too late. The whole surface glowed bright as though its inside had filled with stars and began to shake and rock. They backed up, clinging to each other, but with the crater edge so unstable and Asher unable to run, they were trapped.

Karmi held her girlfriend close and squeezed her eyes shut, hoping against hope they'd survive whatever was about to happen. They tensed, pressed close to each other, and waited.

Nothing happened.

"What's going on?" Asher whispered, peering over Karmi's arms.

"I don't know," she whispered back. Her breath tickled Karmi's neck.

They jolted at a loud click, and a line of light appeared along the surface. It spread out into a square that, with a small hiss, began to open out like a hatch. As they watched with open mouths, some sort of little beast tumbled out, tail flying and claws scrabbling against everything on its way down. The girls backed up in alarm, gripping each other.

The little beast - or whatever it was - righted itself and scuffled around, patting down the earth with its tiny paw pads until it turned its head towards the two girls. It froze and stared at them with wide, star-like eyes. They stared back.

It screeched and hopped around madly. The girls shrieked and Karmi pushed herself in front of Asher, back facing the creature and arms spread out in front of her girlfriend protectively. She shut her eyes, bracing for attack.

Nothing happened.

She glanced back to see the little creature crouched close to the smooth object - which she now realised was its spaceship - and cowering with its paws over its face. The girls glanced at each other then back at the little thing. It peered at them through its claws, twitching. Slowly, Karmi pulled away from Asher to get a closer look at it, crouching down.

"I think it's scared of us."

"Hey, little guy, it's okay," Asher said soothingly, inching forward and crouching as best she could with her hands gripping her cane to support her knees.

The little alien - which was the only way to describe what it must be - twitched and flattened back, then straightened and flattened once more, repeating this action several times as it tore between fear and curiosity.

Asher slowly got closer, wedging the cane into the ground and extending her free hand out with her palm up. The creature watched her, eyes flitting between her hand, her face, the cane, to Karmi, then back at her hand.

She made to move her hand closer and it opened its long mouth to hiss and snarl at her, bristling the spine-like hairs on its body that caught the low light in an iridescent shine. She held still until it began to calm down, tiny sharp teeth slowly vanishing from sight as its flinching body relaxed.

They all held still for what seemed like hours.

After some time it extended its face out, little wiggling feelers on its snout stretched towards her hand. Fingers met warm fur and the creature froze. For a moment Asher thought it might bite her, then it pushed its face forward into her hand, its long, little feelers skimming across her skin.

"There you go, little guy, it's okay," she said gently, relieved beyond herself.

"Thank God, I thought that was going to end badly." Karmi breathed out, peering down at it over Asher's shoulder. "It's like a weird aardvark. Where do you think it's come from?"

"No idea. Some woodland planet I guess. Do they exist? Like desert plants in Star Wars?"

Asher watched it explore her hand and wrist with its feelers. "It's crashed here somehow. I wonder if it meant to do that, or if it was a mistake…"

As though it understood her, it straightened up and made little meeping sounds, bouncing on its hind legs. With a flurry of tiny claws it hurried back to the ships side and tapped the edge insistently, gesturing its head at them making more earnest noises.

"I think it wants us to look at it..." Asher shuffled forwards, gripping her cane securely, with Karmi following up close behind.

They inched close and peered through a slim window into the ship, squinting at the glowing lights of the interior workings. Though it was completely incomprehensible to them, the strange leaking and general mess inside seemed to indicate it had been shaken up badly. The little creature tugged on the loops of their shoelaces and brought them around to see how far the damage had spread.

The other side had a long thin crack running up it the ship's shell, slightly dented and warped from impact. Karmi ran her finger along it and pulled her hand away quickly, skin cut and bleeding. She stuck her finger in her mouth and frowned.

"It looks minor, mostly inside damage," she mumbled.

"Yeah but it can't go out into space," Asher added, leaning a bit to look closer, "it's got to be sealed. Otherwise the vacuum of space will rip it apart." She mimed a head exploding.

"Ew. Grim."

"That's space for ya."

The little creature, ignoring their conversation or perhaps just unable to engage with it, pawed at the crack and looked up at them. It chittered and scuffed in the earth around it, anxious.

"I think it wants our help," Karmi said, "but I don't know what we can do. I didn't even pass physics this year."

Asher looked hard at the length of the cut, then down to her cane. A strip of duct-tape ran up it from when it had been cracked on a previous adventure. "I'm no rocket scientist," she began, "but I might have an idea."

Karmi followed her gaze. "But what about you? If we take it off you won't be able to use your cane at all."

"You can help me get home and fix it again. We have to do something, babe. This little guy has no one to help him get home, otherwise."

Karmi looked a little unsure. "Well, if this is what you want to do..."

As they measured up the crack on their hands and tried to work out if they'd need all of the tape, the alien's ears pricked and it began to make anxious noises. They both stiffened as the sounds of footsteps cracking through branches and leaves steadily got closer. Karmi grabbed Asher and carefully pulled her down, the two girls crouching in the narrow space under the curve of the ship. The little creature, curious and confused, began to inch forward, feelers twitching. Karmi reached out and grabbed it by the hind legs, yanking it back and tucking it under her arm, stifling its squeaky protests.

They held their breaths as someone passed by the clearing some way off, low voices mumbling to each other. A white light flicked past them as a flashlight was waved around, then the footsteps began to fade as the people left.

Karmi let out a heavy breath of relief.

"Why did we have to hide?" Asher asked, voice low.

"That was the local official. You think they'd just let this little thing go? Didn't you watch *E.T.*?"

Asher, who had watched *E.T.* eight times, huffed. "Okay. Fine. But they'd have a better idea of how to fix this ship than us."

"Better a janky ship than a stolen alien."

"Yeah, good point."

They pulled themselves back to standing, the alien very disgruntled at having been restrained without warning or clear reason. They were all, at least, still safe. For now.

"You sure you want to do this?" Karmi asked, looking at her girlfriend's cane.

Asher nodded decisively and together they slowly peeled the tape off. It took both of them to carefully remove it without splinters jabbing into their fingers or sticking to the tape. Soon it was off and Asher's cane was bare, wide crack in the wood bowing it and rendering it totally unusable.

Karmi crouched down, gently ushering the little creature aside. She narrowed her eyes to focus, and pressed the tape, hard and secure, against the crack. With firm scraping motions she flattened it as much as she could, making sure there were no air bubbles beneath it or lose edges. The little creature joined in once it realised what was happening, patting down the tape with quick, hard slaps. When it was covered, the creature pressed its muzzle to the tape and secreted some clear mucus against it, rubbing it in and coating the tape over until it shone and slowly dried hard.

"Gross," Karmi grumbled.

"I guess that must what the rest of the ship is covered in."

"I hate it."

The alien crawled up the shell of the ship like a lizard and jumped back inside. Without wasting a moment it began to clear up the mess, passing them the occasional part or wire to hold while it worked, then snatching them back and putting them where they belonged. It was a strange mix of alien engineering and natural biological behaviours as it used its mucus to seal up splits and breaks in the inside membrane. Karmi looked away for most of it, feeling a bit green around the gills. Asher, in contrast, stared in fascination.

Something in the ship hummed, trembling the ground beneath it, and the alien made a few excited noises. The ship shook a few times, dislodging rocks around it, then settled to silence. The alien poked its head out and chattered at them.

"Any clue?"

"Nope."

It bounced out and ran around to push against the ship, then chattered at them again and pushed again.

"Oh, it's stuck!" Karmi grinned. "We can fix this. Just a regular push-start."

"I'm going to have to sit this out." Asher shuffled back to slowly lower herself against the edge of the crater.

Karmi nodded and crouched down by the underside of the the ship, sinking her fingers into the mud and shoved hard. The ship was lodged tight against the stiff mud. With a mighty, determined heave it jerked once and popped out of its dip in the earth. The area beneath it was sticky and deep green. Karmi wiped her hands on her jeans.

"Guys," Asher whispered from where she was sat, "I can hear people again. Hurry!"

Karmi flapped her hands at the little alien, feeling the alarm start up in her again.

Apparently understanding this time, the alien bounced back inside the ship and started it up. It let out a cheerful squeak and the hatch dropped shut. Like a dust speck in the air, the ship rose up before them, humming and glowing, hovering over their heads.

Asher and Karmi waved.

"Bye bye you weird little guy!"

"Get home safe."

Before leaving, a circle in the bottom of the ship opened up and something long and silvery dropped down. It hit the the earth on its end and wobbled a little, poking out of the ground like a post. The girls flinched back and stared. Without waiting any longer, the ship rose up into the night sky and in a blink of an eye flung itself into the darkness and disappeared into a star, a bright light training behind it that faded even as they stared.

"Well. That was a strange way to spend the night," Asher remarked, a little breathless.

"What is that thing?" Karmi jogged over to the long silvery rod in the ground. "Oh! Oh, wow. Hey, babe, close your eyes."

"Why?"

"Just do it."

Asher sighed and did as she was told. She waited a moment until she felt Karmi's hand pull her broken cane from her fingers. "Hey!"

"Just trust me."

A painful second passed without her support until something firm and cool was pressed into her palm.

"Open your eyes."

She blinked and looked down. A long silvery staff had sat happily in her grip, the surface purple under the dim light. She leaned down on it and it took her weight, squishing a little like it was softening the impact. "It's beautiful."

"No need to worry about the broken one," Karmi said with a beam.

"I guess this is our thanks. It's nice."

"Come on, babe, lets take your alien probe and get home."

"It's not a probe."

"You don't know that."

They awkwardly climbed out of the crater, Asher marvelling at the staff. Once they were back on flat ground they picked their way through the still-damaged forest back to the suburbs. If they squinted when they looked up, they could still see the light trail from the space ship.

As they came to a more sparse area of the forest, a flashlight blinded them momentarily.

"Hey, you two, what are you doing here?"

Karmi raised a hand and squinted at the officers, a scowl on her face.

"We were hunting a fallen star," Asher replied smoothly.

Karmi looked at her quickly.

"Did you kids see anything out of the ordinary?"

Asher shook her head. "Nothing. I guess it was pretty stupid to go looking for that, huh?"

Karmi barely held back her grin.

"Alright, well, you two get home now. It's too late for young folk like you to wander around. Go on. And if you see anything unusual, report it."

"We will."

The two girls headed off as quick as they could until they reached the paved ground of the suburbs, where they quickly fell into giggles.

"Sure hope we don't get into any trouble for this," Karmi said once she'd calmed.

"For what? As far as anyone is concerned, we went on a walk to test my nice new cane."

"Do you think the little guy will come back?"

"I hope so, but this time with a safer landing."

They both fell into giggles once more.

Erode

Emil had never seen sand in his life. Marine pollution had left its mark on the little seaside village. The older locals had watched first-hand their once beautiful home turn into a dump site. The upside was, at least, that no one wanted this.

When the sun rose, before anyone went to their day jobs, before those on the night shift went to bed, they gathered by the sea. Bags, grippers, sharp poking sticks and nets were all kept in beach huts on the shore line. The queues to gather implements were long, but there was always enough. If anything broke, effort was made to fix it or craft a replacement.

Of course some people complained of being too tired to start to early, but Emil had never known anyone to forgo their duty to the village. It was life, routine. He woke up every morning and had his breakfast, then went down to the beach to clean. If someone couldn't make it - being too elderly or too sick - they would do their best to encourage others and suggest new ways of dealing with the bags of litter. Emil, often on his crutches, did what he could when he could.

Bit by bit, he could see the beach changing. Even though new litter was washed to the shore every day, the efforts of the people cleaned it up faster that in arrived, if only just. The containers lined up on the edge of the beach, every day filled with litter to be handled, were starting to look more full than empty.

Emil started his day as usual, comfortably fed and sitting on an upturned bucket as he jabbed at dirty plastic bottles and decanted them into a bag. He didn't wander around like many of the others, but this worked fine for him. He might not cover a lot of area, but the little circle around him would get some serious cleaning.

The wind had started to pick up, making plastic bags roll bounce across the ground like animals running from hunters as the locals chased after them. The waves hit the shore a little harder, forcing the dirty lines of refuse further up the beach. Now and then people would stop and eye the sea nervously.

"Looks like a storm starting to fester," Emil's grandmother observed, voice low and ominous.

"We've had storms before," Emil replied, "it can't be that bad."

"Oh, they can, dear. Just you watch. One like this comes around only a few times in a lifetime, and I hoped I had seen the last in mine. Just you wait."

Emil looked out at the dark clouds on the horizon. He'd known storms to bear down on the village, drowning the roads and blowing the water at every building until it seeped through the gap beneath the doorways. The wind would pull at any nearby trees and make the roof creak. He couldn't imagine what it might be like if it got worse.

They continued to pick at the litter, many continuing even as people made their way to work or home. Emil didn't have any classes, as he was usually homeschooled, so he continued to clean from his bucket. As long as there were adults about to keep an eye on him, he and other kids were allowed to stay for as long as they wanted.

Wind wailed from far over the ocean.

Emil leaned forwards to stab a plastic cup when a sudden gust sent everything around him flying away, tumbling up the beach towards the houses. Another wind spun them around in a little cyclone and cast some bits back out into the sea. Something sharp blew past and scraped Emil's arm, scraping a line along his skin.

He huddled in on himself and headed off the beach as fast as he could, the wind chill stinging and making him more uncomfortable with every second.

By the time he'd made it back home and was opening the front door, the wind was shaking the waves, foam bubbling and frothing off the tips. Trees all down the street had started to bend at alarming angles. The few people still out and about were nervously rushing indoors, clutching their clothes and keeping their heads down. Windows trembled, the house frame creaking threateningly. Even as Emil shut the door it resisted, the wind trying to follow him inside.

He tried to focus on his classes, finger following the words on his textbook, but the rain angrily refused to give him peace. It battled on the roof and drummed on the window. The rumble of thunder accompanied it like some parade turned riot. The shadows that settled over the houses dissuaded him from going out and having a look. He shifted further from the window panes, worried about the damp that had begun to soak through.

It only got worse. That night the door rattled like people were trying to break in. Water squeezed into the house through cracks and gaps, over-filling pots laid out to catch it. The rest warped the ceiling into a bowed, dark, damp patch. The floor bubbled, barely able to hold itself to the ground. Emil clutched his grandmother and wondered if the house itself would fly away and abandon them to the elements. With no other defences, they huddled together on the old armchair and whispered quiet prayers.

When the morning came the storm had passed, but taken with it the illusion of a consistent lifestyle that the residents of the village had grown accustomed to. Emil's home had survived, but others had lost roofs or even the whole side of their homes. Snapped branches and even whole trees were strewn across streets or buried in broken walls. Pieces of homes lay scattered around the neighborhoods.

Most heartbreakingly, the litter containers had been upturned, and all the contents spilled out when the lids had been bashed and broken open. Decades of hard work had been lost in a moment as tonnes of plastic, bundled and sticky, poured out across the beach and got blown into the debris of the village. It was as though no effort had been made at all - as though they had simply just let it build up into a berg. The mess scorned them like some living beast smug at breaking from its cage.

The clean up began - but only within the boundaries of the village. People banded together to clear trees from the paths while others set up scaffolds to patch up holes in homes. Those less physically inclined used buckets to scrape up the deep puddles and toss it towards the beach until it was slowly absorbed into the ground. The elderly and sick were moved to homes that were still stable, checked for injury, bandaged and cleaned up. It would take many days until the village would feel safe and habitable again.

Emil, at a loss, made his way to the beach. No queues lined the plastic carpeted sand. He took his bucket and stick and set himself down to start.

"Oh, darling, don't you bother," his grandmother said gently when she found him. "We've all decided to leave it."

"But we do this every morning."

"Not this morning, dear. Maybe not tomorrow morning either. Or the one after."

He looked up at her, his bag already full. "Then when?"

She sighed and kneeled beside him. "Probably not for a long time. This is too much for one small village to fix."

"We did it before…"

"It took many, many years. And now we may never get back to where we were. There are more important things for us all to worry about right now."

Emil shrugged. "I will still do it. I can't pick up heavy things or fix anything, but I can do this."

She sighed and squeezed his shoulder. "Make sure not to hurt yourself."

"I won't."

She left him to fill his bags. He wasn't sure exactly what motivated him to keep cleaning the sand, other than it was the same routine he'd done every day of his life. With no classes to go to while everyone fixed up the village, he sat and picked litter until his grandmother came to take him home for food.

The next morning he went at it again.

And the morning after.

Time, as it always did, passed over the village. Many houses had been re-assembled, and those not yet finished were stabilised. The road had safely been cleared for use, and the worst of the debris gathered into indoor storage containers.

However, Emil had not made any visible dent on the immense pile of plastic litter. Despite how much he picked at it, plenty was already washing up in front of him to the point that a small ridge had grown. The village rebuilt and returned to a sense of normality, but the shore only got worse.

This didn't deter Emil, as he had not much else to do. As far as he was concerned he was still filling bags. That made some difference.

During their breaks people had started to watch him work.

Pieces of litter sometimes tumbled off the beach into the village, so the locals gathered it up and stuffed it into their own bags. As they picked up the litter, they steadily cleaned closer to the beach. Before they knew it, people had joined Emil by the sea once more, grippers at the ready.

Obviously it wasn't a smooth transition. Homes were still being repaired, and when the regular rainfall passed overhead people had more concerns about water coming through than litter at their doorstep. But there was a clear shifting towards their old routine.

More people joined Emil every day.

Perhaps because of the scale of the disaster, or the amount of supplies that were in demand, but people began to look at the refuse in a new light. Some had started finding new uses for larger sheets of plastic, weaving it together to make waterproof covers for their roofs or bulky seals to go under their doors. Others had constructed windbreakers for the streets, nets to keep the trees from falling on houses, even bigger bags to keep the litter in. Within a week some of the children had raincoats made of sweet wrappers.

It would take many years before clear golden sand shone under the warm sun, but the beach already looked better than it had the day the containers fell.

Emil scooped his first discovery of sand into a jar and put it on the windowsill in his bedroom, motivating him even on his darkest days.

Until We Meet Again

Seconds rumble their way into minutes like old cars on steep hills as you wait, hands knotted together on your lap, in the cramped panini shop you used to frequent as a teenager. Your whole body aches as your muscles fight your instinct to run away. The echoing memory of your of your therapist's voice firmly orders you to stay put. In an attempt to stop yourself from hanging around last minute then cancelling, you'd turned up half an hour earlier and instead stressed yourself out about being alone in public. You had, at least, used the past ten minutes to force yourself to chill out a bit with highly exaggerated optimistic nihilism.

After all, meeting your old best friend after several years was hardly the worst thing you had ever experienced. You knew everything about this girl, things no one else did, like how many of her teeth were real and where her birthmarks were.

Or, at least, you did. Back then. Things change, and circles of trust grow and shrink.

"Sorry I'm late!"

You nearly bolt out of your chair in a panic when your friend practically materialises in front of you. Your eyes jump up to the nearby clock. She's arrived barely a minute after the agreed time. Last time you'd seen her, all those years back, she'd been an hour late. You're so thrown off by this that you almost don't recognise her. Her hair has been pinned into a tidy bun with a little decorative clip and her eyes are bursting from her face with sharp perfectly-even eyeliner.

Looking closer, your heart rate starting to settle, she's very different to how you remember. Once blotchy skin was now smoothed down with products and makeup, dusted with carefully applied highlight and contour. Pale lips usually pressed together in worry were now plumped with rouge. Even her clothes are worn with model-like precision, the sleeves rolled perfectly even and flat, the extra fabric of the shirt tucked into the fitted high waistband of her trousers. If it weren't for the fact you knew her face well enough to carve in marble, you'd never have guessed that she used to be the messy, stressy teenager you grew up with.

You give her a quick smile and a nod, a little mute with surprise.

"Ooh, it's so cute here. It looks exactly the same as it did when we were kids!" She says, her voice sing-songish as she hooks her bag strap on the back of the chair, sitting herself down like she came her every day.

You take a moment to process what she said, then agree quickly, hands fidgeting. She's right. The panini shop still has the same duck-egg green wall paint it's had since the dawn of time, all worn down on the corners and peeling. Even the tables, probably the originals put in when the place opened, are laminated with the same grease-stained marble-pattern cover that had been used on the till counter-top. Judging by the familiar crackling hiss and obnoxiously loud trio of beeps every now and then, even the panini cooker is the same. If you chose to stare long enough at the old furniture and let your mind wander, you could easily pretend you were still fifteen years old sharing a greasy lunch with a classmate.

Except now there was the occasional *ping* of a smartphone. And your back definitely ached more now.

"So, how have you been?" Her tone is gentle, but she emphasises the last word as though she were genuinely interested, her gaze set on you.

You don't know what to say to that. How had you been? Where were you supposed to begin on answering that? You'd struggled through less than a year of university by the time you'd discovered it was actually difficult and definitely not going to get any easier, then proceeded to have a giant meltdown. You'd done a year of socially provided counselling and done a handful of shaky volunteer jobs before getting your first job and then lost it immediately. Since then you'd been on and off somewhere between a handful and a million jobs and not held down a single one of them, while fighting off constant nervous breakdowns anytime a co-worker mentioned how hard they were working on their own university courses or their plans for their successful and prosperous futures. And then you'd suddenly started experiencing longer and longer gaps between the jobs that actually hired you and the pay never increasing despite your years of experience. Then, out of nowhere, you'd been a whole year unemployed and were scraping by off the pennies you had left. Of course you'd managed to scrounge a bit of support from your parents, but under the condition that you got dragged off to long and excruciating mental health assessments. Now you were just left to ruminate while your meds settled back down enough do you no longer wanted to throw yourself into the nearest lake just to avoid the horror of trying to return to another dull and dead-end job and wondering where it all went wrong.

She's quiet as you ramble uncontrollably, following your story even as you weave back and forth in time and add extra side-notes. That at least hasn't changed. She's still easy to talk to, you're relieved to find. Despite her evident success in life she doesn't think herself above you, she's still as good a listener as ever. But you do notice something about the way she watches you, a curiosity on her face like someone visiting a house they grew up in and seeing what the new homeowners had done with the place.

There's a pause after you awkwardly finish where she doesn't say anything. Her gaze drifts and settles on the old coffee maker as it hisses and rattles in a vain attempt to force the last of its life to produce another burned cup.

"I always thought you were going to do well." she says, voice soft. "School always seemed so easy for you."

You barely repress the bitter snort of laughter. You know exactly what she means. Top marks in every class, never needed to study for exams, unconditional offers from every single university you applied to, even a few from universities you hadn't. Teachers said you were gifted, a genius. Your parents thought you'd bring some sort of glory to the family name. The meltdown was a shock to everyone, including yourself. But looking back, the pressure and culture shock had been immense.

"You know-" there's a slight sad laugh to her voice, "I was scared to contact you to meet up." Her gaze is fixed onto the laminated table, fingers laced together against the table edge. "I was afraid I'd see you and you'd be rich and successful, and everything I'd worked hard to get would just be so insignificant next to you. Just like it was back in high school. I had to convince myself that even if you were, it was none of my business. It's hardly like your perfection was an attack on my incapability." An expression flits across her face, as though she had eaten something unsavory.

You don't know what to say. You'd worked yourself up so hard since she'd first messaged you, knowing that even if she was serving in a chippie she'd be doing better than you. Her words throw you completely off course, leaving you mute in the dust. You can see the fine stitching on her shirt, how it's been tailored to fit her, the shine on her lipstick looks expensive and you'd be stupid not to notice that she'd got herself into a healthy shape. How could she possibly think her adult life, so evidently luxurious, could be insignificant? You only stare at her, mouth slightly open.

"It was really, really hard getting to this, you know?" Her hands tense, rubbing the dips between her finger joints. "After all those years on the front desk, I really thought that would be my life forever."

You vaguely remember it. She dropped out of education and worked at the front of some local business checking customers in and out and arranging appointments. That was around when you'd lost touch. Last you heard the place had gone bankrupt and closed down.

"I guess without all that experience I'd never have got this office job. It's dull, though. Really dull. I just sort of type things and sort things and format things and make sure it's all exactly how it's supposed to be." She sighs, heavy and worn down. "I guess it's okay. I can't do anything wrong as long as I smile and make sure everything is working right. Which works for me. I can't let anything out my sight without checking it ten times anyway. I've even been promoted, with a raise." She swallows, lips forced into a stiff smile. "I used to imagine you'd turn out to be my boss or something. I ended up getting- getting really bitter and- kinda resenting you, I guess. But now I've heard what you went through I- I can't believe you just went through all those years alone and I had no idea. I just- let you fall away from me because I thought you wouldn't want me dragging you down." She stops herself with a caught breath, blinking fast.

You let out a breath you didn't realise you'd been holding, and suddenly it all makes sense. The false nails covering rough thumb ends where the white had been bitten down to the skin. Her face scrubbed clear of any imperfection and smoothed beneath natural-looking makeup. The high waisted trousers keeping her stomach as flat as it could, compressing her into a delicate curve. Everything in its place, as close to perfect as it could be. Maintained always. Controlled.

You can see now, why she made it. She didn't have the choice not to, unlike you who had the constant chorus of 'I'm sure you can do it, just like you used to'. For her it was always the uphill climb. You remember the panic she went through every time bad grades came back. Her crying at your house after the final results were handed out. The way she'd work herself up before every exam until she was falling apart at the seams.

But you. You didn't know how to work. You didn't know how to scrape your fingers against stone until you found water. You didn't know how to bleed for your goals. And so when you hit the wall your glass bones shattered.

You were told your perfect world was already built and waiting for you, all you had to do was pick yourself up after this little setback and just go get it. She was told there was no world for her. You fell into the canyon between what you'd known and what you'd been promised. She taped bits and pieces together and spent every moment trying to hold it together.

You hope one day you can crawl back up even if it means bleeding your hands against the cliff face, but you don't know if she could ever let anything go - just in case the tower of cards comes crumbling down.

You reach a hand out and set it on hers, squeezing gently. "You were never dragging anyone down. Not even yourself," you say, voice hushed like you're afraid of anyone overhearing.

She smiles, lips tense and pressed against her teeth, blinking rapidly as she looks down. "I should have been there for you."

"Don't think like that," you continue in that quiet voice, "I didn't want anyone there. I cut you off because I was ashamed. I'm not anymore. I mean, I'm upset about it, yeah, but I'm working on getting back up."

She holds your hand tight, like she's afraid if she lets go you'll fall down again. "I'll be with you this time. And maybe you can come cry at my place for a change?" She laughs a little, short and tense, like it hurts but she doesn't mind.

"I think the last thing you need is all my emotional baggage on your shoulders. You seem loaded enough."

She looks at you with kind eyes. "Let's just put our bags together and share the load."

You laugh this time, a little weak and quiet, but it's the first time you've laughed in a while. It's nice.

She orders a coffee, and it sits there steaming quietly. She buys you one as well and you don't even wait for it to cool, briefly appreciating the burn on your tongue and the full, bitter taste in your mouth. She sips hers, quiet and pensive, then her eyes catch yours and her mouth pulls into a grin. The one you remember, the one that shows the tips of her teeth.

The panini maker hisses and sizzles as cheese spills and burns, and you breathe in the acrid smell you smile back, feeling like teenagers again.

Bernard's Barbers

Bernard's Barbers made an extremely modest business, if you could call it that. It sat at the edge of a run-down little town in the middle of nowhere that rarely ever showed up on a map and no one ever passed through. Bernard worked alone and had the same eight regulars in every few weeks, as well a handful of irregulars to spice things up. The income just about kept the business open - but barely. Bernard rarely saw a profit, but that's just what a small business in a small town was like.

It was a quiet, slow day (as most days were) when the bearded stranger in ragged clothes walked in. Even before he had stepped into the building, Bernard could smell the stench of stale sweat and hair grease that clung to his skin, despite the carefully maintained smells of hair products in the shop.

"Hey, can I get, uh…" The man seemed uncertain, skittish, "a shave? And my hair fixed. I guess."

Bernard nodded and gestured to a chair, then turned to collect his tools. Any customer was a customer, no matter how worn and ragged their clothes may be. Bernard had certainly seen locals in worse condition after a night out.

The man settled himself down, fidgeting with his hands. Bernard wrapped the black cape around him and pinned it neatly at the back, brushing his scraggly hair out the way and ensuring no gaps could allow cuttings to slip under. The man held stiff beneath Bernard's hands, and he wondered if his rather large form was intimidating to this tiny, twiggish stranger. His size had apparently caused some distress among people in the past, but he forced himself not to worry about it too much. It only made it harder to get on with what he enjoyed.

And he really enjoyed - no; loved - his job.

He stepped around to get a closer look at the man's face - worn and overgrown, but not too unlike his average customer. With the focus he had come to be known for by the locals, he chopped the excess beard away and applied a cream diligently to the remaining scruff. The smooth draws of the barber's knife cleared wiry greying hair to reveal smooth forgotten skin. He slowly cleaned the stranger's face inch by inch, blade turning and curving over the rises and dips. He cleaned the hair like a forest being cleared away, leaving hills and valleys smooth. By the time he was done the stranger already looked decades younger. Satisfied, he wiped his knives clean and set them aside.

Next part.

He grabbed a brush and tamed the frizzy, knotted mess of hair down, combed it into controllable locks, sprayed it with water to detangle some of the worst parts, and then began the shearing. Scissors chopped away, thinning the volume and shortening the length until it became manageable enough to begin the fine detail. Fingers for measurement, snip, brush- measure, snip, brush- measure, snip, brush. Spray of water, comb, measure, snip, brush.

He modelled the hair into a neat side-part that shined glossily with a new health.

The sideburns were his masterpiece. Scraped away and formed into perfect faded points either side of the stranger's cheeks. Trimmer hummed and blade dragged as he made them shape a newer, younger face with revitalised energy.

He brought the back into a perfect neat point and cleaned away stray hairs from the neck, making the skin hidden beneath flush pink.

He rubbed in oils and cream, brought new life to the previously haggard face, worked in styling gel that healed the damaged hair and gave it a lively, bouncy tone and a luxurious fragrance. He even took a little time to tidy the stranger's eyebrows, offended by the mar in what was otherwise a perfect head.

The stranger gazed at him the whole while with wide yet murky eyes.

Once finished, he wiped the man's face clean and brushed him off, casting away lumps of matted, dead hair to the ground. He took the cape off and draped it aside to clean off later, then meticulously wiped away any tiny last clipping. Once certain he had sorted it all, he reached for the mirror raised it, showing the stranger his new cut from different angles.

"Wow... I look totally different. I... I really didn't think I could ever see myself like this." The stranger was misty-eyed and voice wobbly.

Bernard set the mirror down and nodded.

"Oh, right, I owe you now. Let's see, how much?"

Bernard looked up towards the prices board and gestured with his head. The man glanced over and his expression slowly fell.

"Ah. Okay. I don't... I don't have that."

Bernard's fixed him with a steady look.

"I- I have..." The man dug in his pockets, stitched up through the battered trousers and clearly expanded inside to allow him to carry more on his person. "Uh...Half..."

Bernard's eyes dropped down to the assortment of dirty coins. He was barely managing to keep the shop open on full price, let alone half. He could lose the business any day. His prices were definitely too low for the work he put in, for the training he'd done, for his years of practice.

But if half was all the man had, it hardly made a difference.

He shook his head and raised a hand, waving the stranger off.

"What? But- but I can still pay half."

He shook his head again and gestured his head to the door as he began to tidy his station.

The stranger stood for a moment, confused and muted by shock. Then, once it clicked, he gave him a wide smile - crooked teeth that needed cleaning and straightening - and tears built in the corner of his eyes.

"You've changed my life. You really have. I'll come back and pay you back one day, I promise."

Bernard nodded. He wasn't sure if he believed it, but he held every promise made to him close to heart.

The stranger left and he began to clean up, once again alone in the barber shop.

The window broke one night, exactly how he wasn't sure, but huge thick cracks branched out across the clear pane and cut through his painted shop-front sign. With not a penny spare to fix it properly, he grabbed some parcel tape from his tiny flat upstairs and willed it not to push through beneath his hand as he taped it together. It held up securely, but he spent the rest of the day feeling phantom glass in his palms.

He managed one whole day of wiping the store down and cutting a regular customer's beard before the uneven light and awkwardly cast shadow drove him into a fit of discomfort. He tore apart cardboard boxes and taped them over the window, boarding it over completely. It was harder to work in the dim artificial light of the old bulb, but it was hardly like he had enough people in to worry about it too much.

He wondered if the boarded window would put off the irregulars and unexpecteds.

A letter arrived from the landlord demanding his late rent. He wondered if he could negotiate for some of it paid now and the rest later - when he eventually had the rest. He had no idea how to go about that. He folded the letter and tucked it away where he wouldn't have to look at it.

Regulars stopped turning up when he expected them to. He polished his blades and lined everything in the shop up perfectly. Business ground to a solid halt. He spent a whole day meticulously cutting every hair on his own head and wondered if the boarded window gave the impression that he had shut down.

It felt like he had.

He had one customer peek a head in curiously.

"We all thought you'd closed," he explained, "not left, we didn't take you for the sort to just run off like that. We figured you maybe just give up on the shop to move onto something else. The guys will be glad to know you're still open, but you'll want to get that window fixed. Looks like a real health risk."

Bernard knew that wouldn't be an option any time soon.

He wondered if he'd have to give up the store after all.

The landlord visited with a scowl on his face.

"I can take you to court for this," he threatened.

Bernard stared silently down at him.

"I want that money, Bernard. If you don't pay up by the end of the month, I'll evict you and your dead-end little business."

Bernard had no response to this.

No regulars came by. Keeping the store open every day became impossible very quickly - the electricity bill was putting him out of pocket.

He closed the shop to think.

The days dropped away, empty and stale.

He'd opened the shop, thinking he'd rather attempt to work with the broken light and stress than not get any work at all. He pulled away the cardboard and stuck another layer of tape on the window to keep it secure, trying to make the shape more block-ish and less uneven. It was ugly, but it'd have to do.

He swept a thin sprinkle of dust from the surfaces and set out all the products he'd need, hoping it would attract his regulars back. As long as he made it look like the place was running fine, surely everyone else would believe that it was fine too.

He didn't have much longer to make the rent. If he didn't make some income soon, he'd be thrown to the street.

As the thought went through his head, a sleek looking car pulled up on the pavement outside. The sight of the clean bonnet filled him with such dread that the car may as well have driven into him. He could only stand, numb and without a plan, as a well-dressed and groomed man stepped out the car.

He wondered what he was going to do. This was the only life he knew. He'd grown up around the smell of aftershave and the soothing buzz of trimmers. He didn't know anything else. This was him.

The man entered the store. He felt himself stiffen, lips pressed firm.

"Ah, you are open? That's good. That's really good. I was worried, I heard you'd closed. This is good." The man seemed a little nervous, despite obviously being wealthy and important enough to use Bernard as his boot cleaner.

He eyed him, jaw set. He had to stay focused in times like this. Pretend like he was in control.

"You haven't changed either. That's good. You have a really comforting aura, you know?"

There was a long pause after this. Bernard had no idea what was going on.

"Uh, I guess you don't recognise me. It's been a while. I owe you for a men's cut and shave."

Bernard felt for a moment like he was pulling open file draws to find information he knew he had. After a minute of kicking over boxes in his brain, he remembered the bedraggled beard and bird's nest hair of the stranger who had come in months before. His eyes widened in surprise.

"I've really shaped up, right?" The man - the stranger - said with an awkward laugh, "I wouldn't recognise me either. It's uh, it's been a busy time. I managed to land a good job I had all the, uh, you know, qualifications and ideas that this company wanted but not the, you know," he waved a hand over his face, "looks. Professional attire."

Bernard felt like he'd been dropped in a foreign country where he didn't speak the language.

"You really helped me out that day. I wouldn't be here now if you had turned me away or called the police or something. You changed my life. I mean it." The stranger smiled, warm and overflowing with gratefulness.

Bernard was only just catching up with the situation. He felt like he should do something, like offer the guy a drink, but before he could decide what to do the conversation took a turn he wasn't remotely expecting.

"Look. I know I owe you like, what, a couple quid? But listen. Listen, can I just… How about I offer you something else, okay?"

Bernard glanced at the door, wondering if someone was standing around with a camera.

"You're an artist. You're a master of this. You're charging pocket change for high-end professional work. That's not- That's not right, man. Look at your stuff, this is all quality. This place is spotless. You can't keep a business open like this. And from what I've heard, you're barely doing that."

He had no argument.

"I think you're incredible. I think you're worth a hell of a lot more than what you have here. I want to offer you something better. How about I take you, I dunno, out to the nearest city. Hook you up with a new, high-end barbers? Get you the work and pay you deserve."

It was tempting, he had to admit, but he'd be leaving his home. He'd be away from what he knew. He'd have to abandon what he'd built with his bare hands. If he left, he'd have to get to know a new place, know new people, and then he really would be in some foreign place where he didn't understand the lingo. On the outside he remained silent, tense, but inside he raged war with his options.

"Okay, I guess this is too much too suddenly, right? I don't - I don't want to freak you out. How about..." The stranger looked around. "How about I help you out a bit here first? I'll get your window fixed and advertise your business to other towns and villages nearby. Hype you up a bit. Get some traffic coming through here. I'll help you with any money troubles for a while until you're on your feet again. You changed my life and took me to places I never thought I'd ever get to experience. I can see that's not what you want me to do for you, but I can at least pay you back half of what you gave me."

He drew in a big, deep breath as he considered it. This was a much more manageable solution to his problems. Even if it did mean a change of pace.

"You seem like you prefer this. Stop me if you don't. But seriously, I'll call someone about your window now. I'll try get a local business, you know? Spread the love around a bit."

This seemed reasonable.

The stranger held a hand out. "You're a good guy, I can tell. To a new friendship?"

Bernard looked at his hand.

"If we shake on it I'll get everything started. You don't have to."

He looked into the stranger's earnest murky eyes and saw the small, unkempt ragged man who had stumbled in, desperately seeking an inch of kindness. He reached out and took his hand, shaking it firmly.

His new friend grinned at him. "I'm so happy we're doing this. I thought about you constantly, and I just need to know you're gonna be okay."

Bernard decided he liked this man very, very much.

The Mane Thing

A distant child's laugh breaks the peaceful silence that blanketed the wide, lush fields. It carries on the breeze that sweeps the grass like rippling water, and tumbles through carefully trimmed bushes. It travels up the narrow stream walled by young trees, drowning the gentle trickling sound, until it meets the cold wet muzzle of a lone horse.

The horse raises its head, ears twitching, tail flicking. It huffs once, ears rotating backwards as it strains to listen. It tenses, restraining the urge to run, not wanting to draw attention to itself. Bolting immediately could attract whatever had made that foreign sound.

Another laugh cuts across the rolling landscape, louder than the first, followed by the sound of breaking shrubbery.

The horse backs up immediately, hooves treading as quietly as it can to avoid attracting attention. It bows its head, tail swishing back and forth in hard jerks, and fixes the gap in the trees with a wide-eyed stare. Bolting would only cause whatever was coming to give chase. It tenses again, flank twitching with anticipation.

A brief silence, then-

The laugh cuts its way up the stream once more, startling the horse, and barely a second later is joined by the sight of a small toddler stumbling to the edge of the stream. It waves its little hands and its little feet bump against stones and sink into the soft muddy bank. The toddler wastes no time in splashing in the clear water, batting it about with unrestrained delight. It takes all the horse's restraint not to run, lest it cause the child to notice it. Instead it waits, ears twitching.

The child grabs a stick and swats the water with the sort of aimless delight only toddlers knew.

So far the child poses no direct threat, but the horse can't be so certain, what with the strange erratic ways of the people who passed through the fields - especially when many showed no intentions or reasoning behind their travels. The younger they were, the more unpredictable their behavior.

Why was this one alone?

The horse turns its head, staring around the fields for a sign of more. One this young was usually with an adult or two, possibly with many more young ones. Its ears turn and strain, all muscles tensing to find signs of more life.

Nothing.

A heavy splash catches the horse's attention, yanking it back to the immediate surroundings. It jolts back, hooves stumbling against the earth, snorting and rocking its head. The toddler, unaware of the horse's distress, flails in the stream, screeching wildly. The horse backs up quickly, scraping the earth with its hooves.

The toddler, apparently unbothered by the sharp edges, grips a jutting rock with its small hands and pulls itself from the water, little dungarees drenched and heavy. The horse watches it intently, stepping back further and ears twitching. Seemingly unaware of the danger it's managed to put itself in, the toddler laughs, high pitched and without restraint. Every wobbly step up the opposite bank sinks its little shoes into the mud. Though no harm seems to have been done, the situation was is no way safe for such a small one.

The horse grunts and takes a few more steps back, discomforted by the slowly approaching toddler tottering over the wet, uneven ground. It huffs, loud and grumbling, hoof stamping on the earth in the vain hope of warding the child away.

The toddler, taken aback by the rejection, whimpers and makes blubbering sounds. Its little hands grasp at air, as though trying to pull the horse closer by invisible rope, bottom lip quaking.

As the horse backs up even more, its ears catch the sound of people's voices on the wind. It pauses and turns its head over to the other side of the stream where the child had come from, ears flicking.

More voices. Older. Loud and calling.

The horse weaves out of the wall of trees and swiftly trots away to avoid confronting the humans, listening out for any more who may approach. Something urges it to stop, though, and it glances back to see the little child fallen in the mud, face starting to screw up in distress. In the distance, two adults wander through the fields. They slowly come closer, heads swaying this way and that, before turning and starting to walk away again. The child, ignorant to its searching parents, grunts and slaps the mud, unable to hear the distant worried calls of its parents over the sound of the stream and breeze in the trees.

The horse grunts and scrapes the ground. It looks to the empty fields ahead then back to the family as they steadily make themselves more divided than before. It huffs and slowly turns, making its way around in a wide arc to avoid the still upset child trying to crawl closer through the mud, and took a moment to step carefully over the stream, ensuring each hoof is secure on firm earth. It awkwardly jogs towards the two adults, head reared back a bit.

They look over, slowing their steps in uncertainty at the sudden, unexpected appearance of the nervous horse. It stops a short distance from them and scrapes and stamps the ground, head nodding. The two adults back up a bit and the horse stamps again, huffing and tail swishing. When this only seems to frighten the two, it turns in a bound of frustration and jogs away towards the stream, grunting.

It slows to a stop a short distance away, the child and adults both in sight. The child managed to pick itself up, steadily getting more distressed as it looks around and wanders in circles.

The adults remain awkwardly still in the empty field, confused and pressing close to each other, grasping hands. The horse stamps and huffs. They give no response.

With no other options it stamps and scrapes on the ground, making sure to keep their attention, then trots across the field to the stream and hops over the water, tail swishing. The adults watch it curiously, so it takes a wide arc around the stream towards the toddler, who has begun making whimpering, blubbering sounds. Thankfully the two adults were now getting the idea, and begin to follow at a cautious pace behind, watching the horse intently. It swings and nods its head at them encouragingly, then trots a bit further up towards the toddler, who's distressed noises were turning into a jerky cry.

The sound catches the attention of the two adults, who freeze and look at one another. A split second later they rush towards the source of the noise, calling out.

The distress and volume of the shouting people mixed with a wailing child's cry was overwhelming. The horse huffs, jerks back and dashes away from the commotion to stand at a safe distance, ears pushed forwards. The adults rush around until they find their toddler bawling on the ground, hands and legs coated in mud and scratches. They gather the child into their arms and whisper soothing words, gentle and loving. The horse observes from its distance, relaxing now that the situation had been resolved.

The family, reunited safely, look over and spot the horse watching them. They stand and begin to approach, quick confident strides. The horse whinnies in alarm and bucks onto its hind legs a few times, stomping and grunting. The family stop, visibly alarmed, and back up. They pause some distance away and watch the horse silently for some time, then steadily back away. Once at a large distance they stop once more and the small child, now calm, turns to wave small, muddy hands at the horse.

It watches them silently for a moment, then bows its head.

The family smile and leave, heading back where they came.

When all falls quiet once more, the horse settles on a soft patch of grass and gazes over the fields. The birds chirp playfully and somewhere far off some other horses slowly graze their way closer, grunting and huffing. The world is in order.

Things That Might Go Bump in the Night

There might have been a ghost in Ro's house. They weren't totally sure. Up until last week, they hadn't really cared much, either. Or, rather, they hadn't had the energy to care much. Slumps came and went seemingly at random, and usually at inconvenient times. Like when ghosts were (maybe) in the house.

The issue with ghosts, and most things in general, was that for Ro seeing wasn't necessarily believing. Things that didn't exist often wandered their way around Ro's vision, sometimes muttering indistinct gibberish. Ro's memory was also pretty poor, so it wasn't easy to say whether they had or had not moved something, or broken something, or if what they had seen had been during waking hours or a dream. This sort of eternal unsureness was something Ro had become very accustomed to in day-to-day life. It wasn't managed at all, but just accepted.

The ghost situation - if it was a ghost - was admittedly different to what Ro normally experienced. Or they thought it was, anyway. The handful times they had caught sight of it while crawling from the bed to the bathroom they had noticed how unusual-looking it was. Unlike the usual hallucinations, the "ghost" didn't have the same watery quality to it, and when it spoke they could just make out words in the whispery, echoing voice. Ro had dismissed it for the most part, more interested in getting a glass of water or crawling to the fridge for snacks, but then their housemate had complained of spoiled food and electronics acting up, and neither of them could find evidence that it was Ro's fault.

There was really only one way to tell if it was a ghost or not. At least in Ro's mind.

Having watched enough ghost hunters in their time, they had a fairly clear idea of what to do. It took a bit of poking around to get the pieces, but soon it was gathered on the kitchen table: An old tin (no match tins were around these days, so instead one that had originally held Christmas cookies); some dirt (from a potted plant mix bought from the store, as the house was on concrete); and some salt (a paper packet taken from a nearby fast food restaurant since no one wanted to waste their own). Once put together it would just be a waiting game where everything relied on a forced sense of patience, and Ro's refusal to second-guess themself into throwing everything away.

Pouring an inch of dirt into the tin turned out to be its own challenge, not just by getting the measurement in the wide base but also just avoiding pouring dirt all over the kitchen floor. Ro was pretty sure the tin still had biscuit crumbs in the bottom corners, but it was far too late. It would be fine.

With their housemate's permission, Ro cleared all the furniture from the living room (a turned over box with a throw on it, and some patched-up beanbags in front of a tv and a play station) to the edges so as to make an empty area in the middle. Ro walked around the awkwardly narrow space a few times, then set the tin firmly down in what was definitely the centre spot.

It sat like a tin of mud in a two-bedroom terrace.

The things (not people - if Ro thought of the hallucinations as people it would really be messed up) stared silently. Not judging, not angry or curious or any other emotion, just neutrally observing the mud tin and the rearranged room. One had oozed itself around a beanbag. Ro ignored them all as usual.

Now it was time to just wait.

And wait.

Of course the waiting didn't need to be done in the living room. That was absurd. Ro retired to their bedroom, a little thankful that their housemate had chosen to spend the night elsewhere. This whole ordeal would probably look really stupid to an observer.

The things, not really observers since they didn't exist, wandered around the bedroom like shadows through a screen. Something about their movements seemed more antsy than usual. There were more of them, too, bumping and blending into each other in a strange depthless crowd. Watching their nervous shaking bodies made Ro a little nauseous, so they close their eyes tight and willed for an empty room.

The next day found the house still and silent. The living room remained mostly untouched, left to ferment - as Ro thought of it - with ghostly energy. Sometimes they would step inside and stare at the tin and its, now dry, dirt. It was hard to judge what was "ghostly energy" or "spiritual presence" when there were already all the stupid shadowy things getting in the way. How was anyone supposed to know when ghost activity stopped if they weren't even sure if it had even started?

By the time the evening rolled around Ro was convinced that the ghost (if it was a ghost) hadn't made any signs of activity since the tin had been put down.

Despite this, they ended up leaving the living room another two days until their housemate got annoyed with not being able to use the play station. Ro was also not finding the situation ideal but also had lost the will to deal with it until their flatmate threatened to spill the dirt on their bed. With an agreement made (Ro actually finished what they started and in exchange no dirt was dropped) Ro sprinkled salt over the dirt and shoved the lid back on the tin tightly, pushing down hard in the hopes it would make a firm seal.

Neither of them were sure what to do with the tin of dirt after. Boxed ghosts weren't listed on the recycling chart, and putting it in landfill seemed a little disrespectful. They debated taking it out to the graveyard to bury it, but the thought of trying to dig a hole at night without being caught felt outlandishly stupid. Neither of them had time to be arrested for suspected grave robbing.

In the end, Ro ended up stuffing it under their bed in between a large stack of old comic books and a box of assorted unidentified wires. They figured they could always return to it on a free day to handle it. To ensure they did actually deal with it and not just leave a ghost stuck under the bed, they went online and ordered a ouija board to arrive within the week. It was cheap and technically a toy, but there weren't many options.

It was about a week later when the salt ring was drawn (in the kitchen where it could be swept up easily). The tin sat on the table, unsuspicious and undramatic, as though it still contained Christmas ginger snaps. The ouija board looked a little bizarre in front of the blue snowflake paint.

Ro lifted the lid of the tin and put the tips of their fingers on the planchette. They took a deep breath, hands already a little sweaty.

"Is anyone there?" They asked the empty kitchen.

Nothing happened. Ro waited, silent and alone in the house. The sink dripped in the slow way that long-term broken plumbing does. The mud remained still and drier than ever. Ro's hands were now sweatier than ever.

Then the planchette moved.

YES.

Ro felt a cold sweat break out on their back and underarms. Something solid built in their throat and their hands began to tremble. They definitely had not moved the planchette.

The ghost - as it may just be - was real.

With an immense effort normally reserved for getting out of bed, Ro pulled themself together enough to focus. Real didn't mean dangerous, it just meant this could be dealt with properly.

"Okay, uh, I'm going to need you to get the hell out of my house in that case." They sounded more confident than they felt.

C-A-N-T

The planchette moving itself around was incredibly discomforting to Ro. "Why?"

S-T-U-C-K

It took an age for each word to be spelled out, which made the response feel far more ridiculous.

"Yeah. Obviously I know that. I put you in there. I mean, like, long-term. I mean, if I let you out of there, do you promise to go away? Will you just leave us alone?"

Stillness.

Ro scowled.

After some time, the planchette began to inch towards the YES. It paused again. Then spelled out F-I-N-E.

Ro nodded, stern and decisive. Then they narrowed their eyes. "Wait. Just to be sure, you're definitely real, right? Like you're a full actual ghost? Or is this me definitely needing stronger antipsychotics?"

YES.

"Yes you're a ghost or yes my brain is a nightmare?"

YES.

"Alright, very funny wise guy. I'm done with your ghosty nonsense. Good thing I prepared for this when I decided to talk to you instead of sneak you into a scrapyard to be cubed." Ro squeaked the chair back and stood, stepping out of the ring to open one of the ugly kitchen cupboards where they kept various bits of junk they had no home for. A bit of poking around finally produced a thick black candle left over from Halloween and an old, tired lighter with the faded name of some hot foreign country printed across it.

It took several scrapes to get the spark going enough to light the dirty wick.

Ro slapped the lit candle on the table, then gave the tin a shake for good measure. "Get outta my house!" They called, "Go on, shoo. Begone spirit!"

It felt very silly shouting at mud.

In an attempt to be more assertive, Ro wiggled the candle about to make more smoke and shook the tin around, dirt falling onto the floor. In a rush of inspiration, they kicked gaps in the salt ring and dumped the dirt out.

Everything was filthy now.

Ro put a hand on the planchette. "You there?"

They stood in the middle of the mess and listened to the silence. Even the weird things had all crouched back, intimidated and waiting.

Nothing.

"Good."

The front door clicked loudly as it was unlocked. Their housemate had come home. A few seconds later she poked her head into the kitchen. "Uh, you okay in here?"

"Zoey! Yep. Just got rid of the ghost."

"And it was definitely a ghost?"

"Definitely. I even asked it to be sure."

"Great. So no more food is going to go off? My pickles are safe?"

Ro sighed, suddenly aware of all the dirt under their nails. "Yes, your pickles are safe and won't grow fungus."

"Good, because you know that estrogen craving is merciless."

"I know, I know. Don't worry, we're ghost-free." She grinned. "Great! Now clean all this up."

Ro looked down at the mud on their feet. "Right. Yeah. I'll do that."

Zoey nodded and backed out to head up to her bedroom.

Ro grinned to themself and looked around. The things had shrunk back, wobbly and watery. Ro brandished the still-lit candle at them. "You guys are gonna get banished one of these days. Just you wait.

They didn't respond.

Ro huffed and blew out the candle, then began the long process of cleaning up.

The Far Away

"Hello, house," Cynthia's mum called as she opened the front door to their new home, signing stiffly with one hand at the same time. She would have done it better had she not been carrying a bag under her arm.

Cynthia, a young girl with her hair in two cute puffs, stepped in and looked around. It wasn't the country estate she had imagined. It wasn't even close to the beautiful, grand houses she had seen on tv and her story books. It was a crumbling old country house with rickety doorways, wobbly floorboards and a twisty staircase that had already lost some steps and spindles. Everything stank of damp and dust at the same time. Every light breeze outside made the house tilt.

"The house doesn't like us," she signed to her mum.

"Don't say that." Her mother spoke and signed at the same time. "We're lucky to have this house. It's bigger than our old house, and it has all been paid for. We just need to clean it up. It's almost perfect."

Cynthia didn't think any amount of cleaning could make this place perfect. In her opinion it needed to be knocked down and completely rebuilt. She didn't tell her mum this, though, it would upset her. Instead she hoisted her backpack with all her belongings in and made the unsteady ascent up the stairs.

The hallway was dark and if she looked closely she could see mould in the corners. She poked her head into each room on her way, heart sinking more and more. Most of them were in a bad state with holes in the walls, dripping ceilings, or windows so broken that leaves had blown in.

After wandering around for what seemed like ages she found a room right at the top of the house at the back with a huge intact round window and a still-standing ornate princess bed. She dropped her bag onto the mattress and flinched back when a huge cloud of dust rose. There was no way this place could ever feel like home.

Her mum came up a short while later and did her best to make it nice. She beat the dust from the mattress and covered it in freshly cleaned sheet, then together they worked to tidy as much as they could. They wiped the surfaces, hoovered all the carpets, mopped the floors and stuffed bin-bags to bursting point with leaves and broken wood. Her mum handled the glass she wouldn't get injured. Everything that needed tools to repair was covered with sheets for a later date.

At the end of the first day Cynthia's room was good enough to sleep in, even if the rest of the house was still cold and damp. She still missed her home, though - her old home. Even if it had been way too small and everything was always broken, at least it was near her friends and wasn't so old that it was falling over. Here felt so strange and hostile, and she would probably have to be homeschooled or travel miles to reach the next deaf school. She lay in bed and stared at the painted ceiling, clutching her bear and counting the cracks.

A flake of paint fell down onto her face.

She blew it off and sat up. With a single swing of her legs she slid out of bed and put her feet into her slippers, glad her mum had warned her of splinters. She padded her way down the dark hall, bear still clutched in her hands, and squinted around in the shadows as she tried to remember where the bathroom was. Her feet directed her around corners, leading her to the end of a long hallway where a cool chill weaved between the walls.

She reached her fingers out and pulled open the carved wooden door, relieved and disgusted to find the massive bathroom. The taps dripped constantly, the floor was stained off-colour despite their earlier scrubbing, and the massive, claw-footed bath had a hairline crack running all the way around it. She stepped onto the sun-faded mat by the sink and reached for a glass. She could have just let the dripping tap fill it, but she didn't want to spend too long in the bathroom so she forced the handle to turn enough to let out a dribbling flow. As she waited for it to fill, she let her eyes follow the strange fairy-pattern tiles all over the walls.

Her cup jerked in her hand and water splashed onto her skin. Her eyes snapped back down to the glass and yelped, dropping the glass immediately.

A little black fish flailed in the sink, gasping. She stared at it with horror, too shocked to do anything. It wriggled and twisted, desperate to get to the trickle of water, tiny fins slapping against the porcelain bowl. She reached out to grab it, hoping to put it back into the cup and release into the pond, but it slipped between her fingers like greasy soap and disappeared down the drain.

A cold sickness began to rise in her stomach. She grabbed her bear and ran, heart hammering in her throat. The hallway was dark and twisty, the rooms unfamiliar and her memories of the day blocked out with panic. She stumbled around, bumping into the wall and stumbling over dips in the floor. One slipper fell off and as she hopped on one foot she was sure she could see eyes staring at her in the gaps in the walls. Tears pricked at her eyes and she wobbled, falling to the hollow ground hard.

She sobbed where she lay until gentle hands gathered her to sit up. Her mother's face came into view, blurry behind a wall of tears, obviously still half asleep. Without hesitation she held her tight, sobbing against her shoulder as her mother rubbed circles onto her back. When she eventually settled, her mother pulled away just enough to ask what was wrong.

"I don't like it here," she began, "there are fish in the taps."

Her mother's brow furrowed in confusion. "Say again?" She asked, wondering if she had misunderstood her daughter's frantic, dirty hands.

"There are fish in the taps," she signed again, sharp and clear.

"Darling," her mother responded gently, "are you having nightmares?"

She shook her head and buried her face against her mother's shoulder once more, not wanting to talk. Eventually her mother pulled away again to wipe her tears.

"Do you want to sleep with me tonight?"

She nodded, sniffling.

Her mother gently took her hand and lead her inside her new room, mostly empty and in desperate need of decoration, then pulled her into bed. She held her close, one hand on the back of Cynthia's head to sooth her, and quietly rubbed her back with the other until she fell asleep.

The next morning was proof that it hadn't just been a nightmare. Fish fell from every tap, and weird sludge seeped from the shower head. Little frogs had broken in downstairs, bouncing around the kitchen and living room. The bin bags had all been ripped open and the mess inside strewn along the stairs and hallway.

Cynthia sat at the dining table with a bowl of cereal and watched a few rescued fish swim in lazy circles in a large glass jug. Her mum called a plumber, a whole list of other people to call on a notepad in front of her. It would take weeks to get their new home in shape, and even longer if it meant creatures had made nests in the ancient house. Her mum was convinced that it had just become infested while it was left empty - but Cynthia couldn't shake the memory of the eye in the walls. It didn't feel right. No matter where she went in the house, she could feel the crawling feeling of being watched. And not by some animal.

"I've done everything I can for now," her mother signed, chest falling with a sigh. "Would you like to go outside and look around the garden? We could plan to put a swing or garden table out there."

Cynthia brightened considerably at this - their old house hadn't had any sort of garden at all. The door had opened onto the street and the back had been a small concrete area with huge walls around it. She'd always dreamed of sitting on a swing under a clear, starry night.

The garden was more of a wilderness with gnarled trees and unkempt bushes all over the grounds. The grass was too long to walk comfortably, wrapping around their ankles. Here and there some tree stumps poked out between the green blades. The undergrowth rustled as little creatures darted through the gaps to escape their approaching feet, flashes of tiny bodies and tails between the leaves.

Approaching the far edge of the garden Cynthia spotted a large growth of mushrooms and crouched to investigate the wide bell-tops. She shuffled to follow the thick trail of them for several feet until, with a jolt, she realised it surrounded the entire house in one huge fairy ring. She gazed at the house, a breeze making the grass tickle her ankles.

Someone grinned at her from a window.

She jumped to her feet, feeling cold sting at her edges. The person had vanished, but she knew what she'd seen.

She was dragged from her thoughts by her mother tapping her shoulder. "This tree looks strong, we could put a swing here."

She only nodded at her mother in response, no longer caring about her past fantasies.

The people in hard hats and protective jackets who came to the house to fix all the damage did what they could, but tools kept vanishing and their hard work undid itself. At some point a light fitting nearly hit someone on the head, and they called it a day until they had someone else to come and re-assess the damage.

Pest control were called, but surprisingly not a single nest was found anywhere. Gaps were filled and some deterrent traps dropped, but Cynthia suspected it wouldn't last.

The house was deemed safe to live in, despite being so run down.

Cynthia didn't believe that one bit. Her mother was similarly skeptical, but they had nowhere else to go. They made the tireless effort to tidy and clean and fix, trying to make the house feel like a home. It was a thankless task, as furniture kept moving from where they put it and things just went missing despite having been seen a second before. Cynthia could feel eyes on her everywhere in the house.

It was a few days later when Cynthia was temporarily left alone while her mother went to pick up some groceries, leaving the orders to keep an eye on everything for the next half an hour. As soon as the front door closed, though, she knew she had no intention of peacefully looking after the home.

She marched through the hallways, seeing things skitter through the walls and between the floorboards. She swallowed hard and stood in the main living room at the centre. After a pause, in which she could feel everything holding its breath as it watched her, she raised her hands and waved, hoping it would catch attention.

Nothing happened for a moment, then the walls and floors shook as things rushed through the house. She gripped her own sleeves tight, arms wrapped across her chest, and swallowed hard. Wind burst through the windows, bringing in dead leaves with it, blustering her about. She held her ground. Steadily debris and dust gathered in front of her into a human form.

A young person appeared, neither a boy nor a girl, and smirked wickedly.

Somehow, now faced with the threat in a way she could understand, she felt less afraid. This was a kid, just like her.

"Who are you?" She asked it.

The kid - or spirit - stared at her unblinkingly.

She signed again.

Its face stretched into a mischievous grin before its form began shaking, leaves peeling away from its body. Before she could do anything it bust apart into wind and leaves once more and blew past her, pulling at her hair and clothes. Something stuck in one of her puffballs.

She turned to see the spirit again, sniggering behind her.

"Who are you?" She asked it again, irritated.

It stuck its tongue out, made of leaves and twigs, then copied her sign back at her mockingly.

She bit her tongue to stop herself poking it out in response. Instead she decided to answer the spirit. "My name is C."

The spirits expression chained into one of curiosity, surprised that the gestures had changed. It attempted to copy the gesture, though smaller and with less conviction.

She simplified it, pointing just to herself then saying "C," and repeating the motion. Once the spirit seemed to understand, she pointed at it and then asked, "Your name?"

The spirit didn't respond immediately, crossing its legs in the air and thinking. After a moment it zipped close to her and plucked the leaf from her hair, then pointed at it then itself.

"Leaf?" She asked, then pointed at the leaf and repeated the gesture.

The spirit - Leaf - nodded enthusiastically. Then, as though spurred on by their conversation, it began to gesture to things in the house, then to itself. The walls, Leaf. The roof, Leaf. The floor, Leaf.

She watched until it settled, then nodded. She made a wide sweeping gesture to the whole house, then pointed at herself and said, "This is mine too."

Leaf scowled and shattered to a thousand pieces, blustering through her once more and shaking the house. The doors swung open and a stream of leaves and twigs tumbled out to the backdoor. Cynthia put a hand over her eyes to keep them protected and ran outside after them, watching Leaf reform in the garden, larger than before.

"We have to share," she told it, bottom lip stuck out.

Though it couldn't understand her, her attitude was enough to rile it up once more. With a huge whirlwind it pulled at the grass and the leaves, yanking her clothes and tugging at the ties in her hair. A branch, snapped from the trees, caught her face as it blustered past and cut a line across her face. She stumbled back, clapping a hand over it, gasping and eyes pricking with tears.

She turned on her foot, back to the spirit, and ran. The wind settled and stopped pulling at her, but she kept running. She slammed the door behind her and ran up the rickety stairs and along the creaky hallways all the way back to her bedroom. Sniffling and hiccoughing, she huddled against her bed and picked pieces out of her clothes.

Her door opened but she ignored it, wiping tears and blood off her face. Without her mother home, and with no way of talking to her friends back home, she was very much alone.

Even here she wasn't wanted.

One of the boxes of her belongings - still unpacked in the hopes she wouldn't have to stay - fell off her table. She frowned and sat up, glaring down at Leaf who had reformed on her floor, poking through her stuff. She kicked out at it, but it avoided her foot and picked up a framed picture. It was her school year photo that had been taken before she left.

Leaf pointed to the school building in the photo then to her.

She shook her head. "Can't go back."

Leaf tapped the photo again and she shook her head, scrunching up her face. She buried her face in her crossed arms, curling tight.

The breeze of wind told her Leaf had left.

She sat alone for a while.

After she had cried herself tired, she raised her head and wiped her face. She blinked until her eyes were no longer blurry, and noticed there was a long trail of leaves and sticks leading out of her room. She sighed heavily and dropped from the bed, picking up the mess. To avoid her mother's stern telling off more than anything.

The trail led her through a part of the house she hadn't paid much attention to, the rooms too run down to stay in. She followed the trail into a room that had been almost entirely ruined, save for a single painting that Leaf was staring at. She gingerly made her way across the damp floorboards to look at it.

The rich landscape stretched across the canvas, lush and bright. She glanced aside and realised that it was the same as the landscape out the window - but now dull and littered with houses.

She pointed at the painting, then at Leaf. "Is this your home?"

Leaf nodded, understanding her beyond sign language.

She reached up onto her tiptoes and took the painting down. Without explaining herself to Leaf, she rushed downstairs to where the front door was opening, her mother home. She stopped in the hallway with the painting in her hands. Before her mother could raise a hand to greet her, she was pushing the painting at her.

Her mother awkwardly set aside a large potted plant she had bought to look at the painting. "Is this here?"

She nodded.

"This is pretty. Should we plant some trees in the garden?"

Cynthia nodded again, beaming.

Her mother smiled and leaned over to kiss her brow. "Help me get everything inside. Were you lonely?"

"No," she signed back, "I had fun."

Her mother pulled a twig from her hair. "That's good," she replied, then frowned at the sight of the scratch. Seeing Cynthia wasn't too distressed, she kissed her cheek, then nodded to the door where the car boot was propped open. "Come help."

As Cynthia put the painting against the wall and stepped out, she could see little leaves settling around the potted plant in a delicate ring.

The Grove of the Ancient Sage

The Grove of the Ancient Sage is located far from any map lines, completely off-set from the foot-worn pathways of the common person who treads off the marked trails. In fact, it can only be located by those who know how to look, but have already become long lost.

It was this knowledge, and complete and utter hopeless confusion, that resulted in Shell crunching through the undergrowth one foot at a time. Her long cloak kept snagging on branches, dragging twigs and leaves along behind her. She had been wandering for hours.

The air was still around her. Thick. Too heavy for the wind to move it, too stifling for birds to fly. Only down by her feet did any creature move, crawling and skittering over her boots, unseen where they scratched around in the earth. Sometimes, if she strained her ears enough, she was sure she could hear whispering in between the branches.

She paused and pressed a trembling hand to the bark of a tree, feeling the weight of its tired centuries beneath her fingers. She slowed her breath, body winding down to mimic the ancient life flow of the tree, heartbeat reaching a standstill. In the second of coma-like peace the tree spoke to her in a gentle whisper, telling her the way.

She breathed in and everything returned to normal.

Things were alive here in a way they couldn't be elsewhere.

She continued on, twisting her neck to look through gaps as she searched the unfamiliar forest. Each wary step only seemed to take her further and further into tangled weed and wiry branch. The trees tightened and loomed overhead, her every movement limited more and more as she crawled in the narrow spaces between tree trunks and pushed through thick bushes. A snapped branch caught her neck and scratched it up to her ear, causing blood to spill. She hissed in pain, losing her footing and stumbled over a large stone. Her body collided against another tree.

I'm lost, she thought. It was hard to admit to herself, even after how long she had been out here, but it was true. It was more than just wandering in unknown grounds without any direction in mind, twisting through the nettles, paying no heed to where she went nor where she had been. She was deep in the middle of nowhere with no way out. She was more than lost. She was stranded.

It was in this moment of hopelessness, rubbing her neck and smearing blood across her palm had been pulled out, that her eyes settled on a series of knots in the branches. Several trees had grown close to each other, curving over and twisting tightly to make a high archway. As she dragged herself towards it, she ground became less cluttered with bushes and undergrowth, making a small clearing. Even the smaller trees and branches had curved out of the pathway.

She paused for a brief moment, having to control her heartbeat once more. Then, with a shaky breath, she began along the clear path.

At the end of this sheltered pathway the grove waited. Its roof was buried under thick foliage, and the little round door stood slightly ajar with cozy light and spicy smoke trickling out. Shell sped up as she got closer, gratefully breathing in the warmth. The door opened wider as she drew close, inviting her into the shelter like a mother welcoming home her first-born.

Stepping inside brought back welcome memories of her childhood, entering her nana's home to find hot food and a dancing fire. The grove was much the same - happy fat flames beneath a deep-bellied pot. Something herbal bubbled away while a number of cats, old and young alike, lay about the orange glow and purred. The Sage was comfortably sat in a corner, huddled into a mass of bushy plants wrapped around a softened tree stump as a makeshift seat, carefully embroidering onto the end of a long piece of cloth. She could have grown from one of the trees outside, her body was so creased and gnarled like bark. But her eyes had a kindly sparkle to them that chased away any fears of the dark woods.

"Wise Sage?" Her voice was barely a breath.

The elderly woman looked up, hands not stopping from their task, like an automaton. "You've finally arrived. Sit. Rest. You've had a long journey"

Shell seated herself on a wide branch that stuck out from the bushy walls. Despite its appearance it was quite comfortable, devoid of sharp edges that would poke her. Moss had grown along the bark and formed a soft padding.

The Sage squinted at her silently for a moment, then tutted. She reached out and pulled a rolling table covered in jars and tins towards her. "You're hurt. Here." She lifted a lid and scooped green paste from a jar. Without any explanation she reached over and pressed the paste into the still bleeding cut.

"Ouch!" Shell flinched back raised a hand to cover the stinging wound, now sticky with the green gunk.

"Don't wipe it off," the Sage warned, "it will heal you by nightfall."

She lowered her hand reluctantly, teeth gritted against the pain.

"What brings you to my grove? Rare one so young wanders into the lost lands." The Sage picked up an old tea pot that had been gently steaming on a low table at her side. She poured its contents into a mug hidden amongst the jars, then handed it to Shell who took it gratefully.

"I seek guidance. It is not just these lands that have become lost, leaving us to wander them, but my way has become lost too. And so I am wandering through life without guide."

The Sage hummed and drank her tea. "I, too, have found myself lost on the long road. Many times."

Shell's eyes widened. "But now you are a great Sage. You must have been very gifted to overcome it."

The Sage hummed and fixed her with a stern look. "Sage is a hard-earned title, not an honour given one. I was not born with insight and knowledge that I have today."

Shell nodded quickly, realising she must have said something quite insensitive. "I understand, you worked hard and overcame a lot to earn your respected position. But currently I find all my hard work is getting me nowhere. I push myself and push myself, do everything I am capable of, and I go unrecognised and unappreciated. I feel I have made a mistake to even start."

"Starting anything is never a mistake." The Sage carefully settled her tea on her lap. "You are young. You need not rush to greatness so fast."

"If I do not start now and make my mark while I am young, how am I to succeed as I get older? How will I make my mark to guarantee my future?"

The Sage quietly drained her mug, then refilled it from the teapot. The long stretch of silence between them felt like a slow exhale. "You will live a very long life, as I have, and do many things, as I did. These things will not take part in a five-year span. They will happen over decades of tries and failures and smatterings of success."

Despite the comforting atmosphere and the assured tone of The Sage's words, Shell still found sparks of anxiety flaring up inside her. "But so many others have succeeded at a far younger age than I." She blurted, gripping her mug of steadily cooling tea.

The Sage gestured for her to drink. "And even more have not," she countered, "If we continue to put ourselves against each other, none of us will get anywhere. All you can do is measure yourself against who you used to be."

"I used to be happier."

The Sage watched her carefully. "And why did you stop being happy?"

She shrugged and took a heavy breath. "Too many responsibilities? It's better when you're young, being cared for and still learning the basics. Now I feel like I've learned all the wrong things."

"Not true at all. You are simply not at the stage where they will apply. No learning is without benefit. All education is beyond value. Anything you do not yet know you have all the time in the world to learn."

"But my responsibilities-"

"You can learn as you go." The Sage gestured at her cup. "Drink up before it goes cold."
She nodded and sipped the tea. It was lukewarm. She hastily drank more.

The Sage watched her thoughtfully. "When I was your age, I was not in an ideal position. I sometimes refer to it as when I walked with the wrong body and wore the wrong name, but in reality it was body I had to learn to develop, and the name I could chose to change. I felt in that moment of discovery that I was many, many years behind my peers who knew themselves so well."

Shell nodded as she listened, still drinking her tea.

"I had to learn many new things about myself, and about where I was in the world. It was this change in my life that helped me learn to see inwards and know what I truly wanted to be. This new insight I could apply to everything I came across in life. Self-reflection and introspection is the greatest wisdom of all, some say. If you understand yourself, then you understand the world.

But then the deep winter came, and I lost a close personal friend. The grief stayed with me for many years, and even now during quiet, dark moments I feel that hole in my heart. I was without a part of myself, and so I became listless and unmotivated. I went days doing nothing. My friends and family became distant. At one point I thought I saw the end of my life."

Shell lowered her tea, heart aching at these words. "Your tale is so sad. I'm deeply sorry for the loss you've suffered."

The Sage smiled, and for a split second she was no more than a tired, elderly woman. "Many are, and will continue to be - as with all losses. Life can be cruel, and all we can take from it is the tools to go on. I did not need such a grief to become a hardy person, but it was how I learned it nonetheless. I started with small, simple things and worked myself up to being able to go on - and celebrated every little victory. I imagine my friend watched me from the other side and was proud to see me get going again." The Sage smiled at this.

"But... Surely this put you behind your peers?" Shell asked, turning her cup around in her hands.

The Sage nodded. "Oh, you could say that, yes. I had lost many years to grief and sadness so deep it was more me than my bones. But I was starting again - and that was more than enough. I was determined to get on my right path, and be kind to myself.

"Our concepts of ahead or behind, they are meaningless. There is no race. If someone falls down and gets back up again, they have developed a new strength that others may not ever know. We do not live life on some long path, but in an ever-widening world.

This understanding was necessary to my healing. Grief and loss had been so cruel, I had no need to make it worse for myself.

"So I did only what was good for me. If I pushed myself too hard I became lethargic and upset, so I worked only what I could. I took hobbies that made me feel accomplished-" she held up the beautiful embroidery piece she had been working on, "once you understand that creating something new means creating anything, you can have the world at your hands. I have embroidered many cats now, and no one has the right to tell me to stop." She chuckled to herself.

Shell sighed appreciatively. "That sounds wonderful. I wish I had some sort of hobby I could do - but I'm no good at anything."

"And neither was I. But as I said, starting something is always a good idea. I started many things - cooking, sewing, cat breeding, singing… I would like to have done more physical things, but my lower body steadily became weaker over the years." She shrugged a little. "All the more reason to focus on what I could do. Those made me happier than anything."

Shell smiled. "It's all worked out for you, then."

"So it has. And I did not think it would. In fact, I retreated out here when I found the towns too hostile to stay in. My bones ached and my body became weary. I started so many tasks over the decades, learned so much and had so many responsibilities that it nearly made me lose myself again. So, I took what I could and retreated in the hopes of making a meagre living alone. Little did I know at this point I had such experience that some would come seeking my advice - and unfortunately sometimes some would come to exploit me." The Sage smiled sadly. "Now only those truly lost can find me."

"Do you not miss your old life?"

"Sometimes. But I lived enough of it, and these woods are a kind home. My cats are happy and warm and judge me only by the love I give them. Some say happiness comes from family or friends or wealth, but my happiness comes from animal companionship, a good meal and a completed embroider. When you separate yourself from others, you realise that happiness is not a social standard, but a personal one."

Shell nodded. "Thank you for your story, wise Sage. It is good to know that not everyone who has earned the title was a gifted child that grew into a gifted adult."

The Sage laughed. "Oh no, not at all. I struggled to learn the first lessons. No. I learned through my own means. I am Sage not from an innate all-knowledge, but from what experience I have gained wisdom from. Good experiences, bad experiences, they are all something to learn from. Experience is not a job or a class, but a just another dimension of life."

Shell nodded and finished her tea, now barely warm. Dregs gathered in a neat circle at the bottom. "You have been truly helpful. I think I have what I need to start sorting my life."

"You always did," the Sage said gently, "all you needed was a break."

She nodded and began to stand, brushing moss from her cloak.

"Before you go, do take this."

The Sage carefully tied a knot in the thread and bit it, then shook out the embroidered cloth. She gestured to Shell, who leaned down to let the Sage wrap it around her head and neck, worn fingers carefully putting it into place. Shell reached up to take the corner into her hand and look at the embroidery.

"This cat... Looks just like the one I had when I was a child."

The Sage nodded. "To remind you of times when you were happy, and to keep you on the right track."

"But... How did you know?"

The Sage's eyes glimmered. "Some stories a Sage can never share."

Shell left the grove, holding her new scarf tight. As she exited the clearing, she had a sudden thought, and turned back to return. To her surprise, the grove had completely vanished - no longer accessible to her. She understood and swallowed hard, then walked in the direction she now knew to be the way home.

Sticks and Stones

A curse from the Stone Witch could haunt a person for all eternity, following them even after death. Kai was direly unfortunate to have ended up on the receiving end of one so young in his life. In a desperate attempt to save himself he had offered his services to the witch, hoping that if he won her favour she would eventually lift the curse and free him. Several years passed since that moment.

Today's needlessly impossible task took him out to the stone hills with a wide, flat saucer to collect water. There was a single stream a few miles away, deep into the hills. Calling it a stream was generous, as it was barely a trickle of water spitting through the dry cracks. Often it would be clogged with stones, grit and dirt that made the water bitty and grey. Sometimes it would dry up entirely, the only sign of it ever existing being the dark smooth stain on the rock below.

Kai remembered the way to the stream very well, having to walk the route at least once a day to get a drink. He approached the piddly little drip of water and reached a scarred hand out to scrape his battered nail against the gap, trying to clear away some of the dirt and stones away. It never did a massive amount of improvement to the water flow, but it did at least guarantee it wouldn't clog up.

He held the flat saucer beneath the water and watched the droplets plink onto the surface, steadily gathering in a shallow puddle. If he was clever about it, he could fill it enough but not let the water touch the edge, which would stop it spilling when he carried it back.

As droplets tapped and tinkled against the surface the little orchestra was filled with the additional instruments of hard pebbles and sandy grit bouncing and settling in the puddles. Kai waited until the sounds became muffled by the shallow pool filling, before pulling the saucer away to take back to the witch. He gazed down at it, head ringing with the sounds of falling stone.

The pebbles sat in the saucer like a pond bed, dirty clumps on the clean surface. There was no way he could bring this to the witch. She wouldn't like it one bit. He'd have to clear out the dirt and bring it back as clean as possible.

Kai placed the saucer down and crouched beside it. One by one he began to pick out the larger pebbles, before moving on to smaller ones. The pebbles themselves were in fairly small amount, and easy to take out and discard. The real issue was the smaller pieces: little chips and bits of grit floated in the water. No matter how carefully Kai extracted them the water still stuck to his fingertips in droplets. By the time he'd cleared out the worst of the debris, he'd also shaken half the water into damp patches around him.

With a deep, resigned sigh, he began to fill the water again.

It took well over an hour to clean the water enough to be satisfactory, the ground around him dark and wet. The tips of his fingers had wrinkled. Steadily he lifted the plate, breath held in case it might destabilise him somehow, and took slow steps back to the grove. The shallow water trembled ominously. Little droplets escaped a few times, leaving a speckled trail behind him all the way back to the witch's cave.

As he passed through the large stone entryway, his gaze dropped down to the thin blanket on the floor. The witch had been very kind lately; before she had made him sleep outside, but now he was allowed to sleep in the doorway with something to cover him. If she was in a good mood, he would even be allowed to sleep just inside the hallway.

"What took you so long?" She scolded when he approached. "And what is this? Dirty water?"
"I collected it from the stream, as you asked," he replied timidly. "I'm sorry. You're right. It's not good enough."

"No, it's not. It really won't do." She sighed heavily, whole body sinking into her throne. "Well, all is not lost at least. I had a backup plan in case you failed me. Which you inevitably would." She took the saucer from his hands, letting the lovingly collected near-clean water spill off and splash to the dry floor. She held it out flat as she picked

up a large jug of perfect, clear water beside her chair and poured it onto the saucer. "There. Isn't that much better?"
"Yes, of course." He nodded. "I'm sorry I failed you."

"Maybe this will be a lesson to you. Don't drag your feet and only give a job half your effort, then you might actually be rewarded for it."

He nodded again quickly, biting the inside of his lip.

"If you're going to be such a constant disappointment I'll begin wonder if you want freeing at all? They won't take you back at the village, you know. Not with your awful curse about you."

He lowered his eyes to the curse mark on his wrist. "I will learn to do better."

"Good." She drank her water quietly, then waved a hand at him. "Go away, now. I want some peace. Make yourself useful and polish the walls."

He bowed his head and scurried away.

The stone walls were completely smooth and shiny, like mirrors. It already reflected clear and sharp before he even started on it, not a bump or chip in sight. The witch liked to gaze into it when she was alone, admiring everything she'd made for herself. It never once actually needed polishing.

No one else lived in the Witches Grove. Without Kai there, she would be very much alone. Even the villagers, who were normally a welcoming bunch, would have nothing to do with her. The stone hills isolated her permanently from the world.

Kai stared at his reflection, hand slowing to a still. It must be a horribly bitter and lonely life living in a cave, alone and shunned from society. He stared at the curse mark, and thought about how willing the witch had been to let him stay.

Failing to meet one of her standards wasn't going to get him anywhere, but if he met a standard she had never set in the first place might actually leave an impact.

He hurriedly finished polishing the wall, knowing it made no difference, and slipped out of the cave as silently as he could manage. While he technically was under no obligation to hang around, leaving without permission or orders still felt dishonest. He held his breath for extra safety.

Nothing really grew on the stone hills, just the occasional scrappy weed or sheet of lichen peeling from the rocky edges. There were, however, the rare little flowering plants that tucked themselves where the grit became fine dirt, facing the sun. Kai had seen them out on his errands, but never thought to pluck one from its nest.

Now he found himself gripping tight to a dangerously angled ridge. The drop wasn't too far down, but the bottom was littered with sharp, spiked rock. A single flower, petals broad and bright, stretched out from the ridge with a confidence that the other plant life couldn't compare to. Kai felt a little pang of guilt for having to kill it in its prime, but nonetheless edged closer with a hand extended.

His fingertips brushed the stem a few times, making the flower bounce its head. He stretched further, fingers straining, and managed to catch it just between his nails. With one quick jerk he ripped it out of its crevice.

The flower flicked out from between his fingers.

He fumbled, hand flapping and fingers clawing wildly to catch a grip on the stem. Sweat beaded on his skin.

He just managed to secure hold of the flower, palm sweating as he tried not to crush it. He jerked it close to his chest, then edged back to safety. His blood screamed in his ears.

Feet stumbling over themselves he half sprinted back to the cave, trying to calm himself down as fast as he could.

Now the scary part began. How to present it?

He couldn't bring himself to just give it to her. Interrupting her was one thing, but to randomly hand her a flower on top of that made it a big risk. She would probably mock him and suggest he'd developed some sort of Stockholm syndrome.

In the end he decided to present it with her dinner, which he would obviously be expected to prepare. He poked around the kitchen until he found a small pot that could hold the flower, and waited for the evening when the orders came. He wished he'd had the sense to get some water for the little thing, as it was starting to wilt already. The stem drooped and petals wrinkled at the edges.

He put his full effort into dinner, though it would never reach her expectations. It was always worth giving it his best shot, just to ensure she didn't totally hate it. He chopped everything as evenly as possible, and fine as he could with a blunt knife. Everything was taste-tested three times before he was convinced it was as perfect as it could be, though it sometimes seemed that the witch had a more sensitive palette than he. With absolute care each dish was set out on an ornate slate tray, polished to a glowing shine. The potted flower sat as a sweet, delicate centrepiece.

He paused before leaving the kitchen. Deep breath in. Slow breath out. Then marched into the dining room to present the dinner at the great dining table.

She eyed the flower suspiciously. "What is that?"

"I picked a flower for you."

"Why?"

"I-" His throat caught for a second. "I thought you might like it."

She took the somewhat listless flower from its pot and rolled it between her fingers, then tossed it at him with a flick of her wrist. "Is this all you think I am worth? What a ridiculous waste of time. If you must decorate, make it a bouquet! It can't be that hard."

He flinched back dropped his gaze down, hands shaking. "Sorry."

"But," she relented with a heavy sigh, "I suppose I appreciate the thought - though a bit pathetic. Make the effort next time you decide to surprise me, would you?"

"Of course." His voice cracked.

"Now go away. I want to eat alone."

He scurried out of the room.

Kai sat against a polished wall and nursed a bleeding wound after his latest attempt at making the witch smile. The wild dogs of the stone hills were extremely vicious, and they had not appreciated him stealing a pup. He had no idea where it had gone - probably ended up somewhere in the witch's chambers being fed something strange.

His gaze settled on a sheet of notes pinned to the wall. It was a list of items he needed to get from the village. He swallowed and took it down, figuring it was a good idea to grab some fresh bandaging sooner rather than later, and then he could kill two birds with one stone. He briefly wondered if a dead bird might actually entertain the witch.

It was always a long journey down the hills, and rough on the feet. The nearby village, though small and rural, was often bustling with life. There had never been a dull moment while he had lived there. It felt so alien to him now.

He kept his cloak on the whole time, hood low over his face. Many of the villagers knew he worked for the witch, so kept a suspicious distance. Even merchants at the market stands and stores kept their interactions stiff and limited. All these people had known him once, even been good friends, but now the great weight of the witch's curse hung between them. Kai couldn't blame them.

Having finished the list in good time, he perused a shelf of ointments at a medicinal stall. He kept his wounded hand kept a safely tucked away as he read each label, not wanting to spread any infection. Price was more important that effectiveness right now. He'd used his own money to pay for everything, of course, and now it was starting to run a bit thin.

"You out buying for the witch?"

He looked up quickly and met the bright-eyed gaze of the young man who ran the stall. "Yes."

The young man nodded. He seemed comfortable being the sole person in charge of all the medical wares, despite being about Kai's age. "Thought so. I've seen you about. What do you need? I can get you specific amounts."

Kai shifted, a little nervous at the attention. "I just need something to clean a wound."

The young man straightened up, startled. "The witch is injured?"

"N-no. It's for me."

He blinked, then reached out a hand gestured for him. "Let me see, I can probably sort it right now for you."

Kai edged closer, skin prickling with nerves, and held his hand out. The other man took hold, firm and steady, and pulled away the dirty bandages. The wound was still fresh, the edges red and irritated looking. With a nod and a quick mumbled word, he took a soaked cloth and wiped it over the cut, clearing it out and leaving it raw red. Kai hissed and tried to pull his hand back, stinging pain making his eyes water, but the young man held him firm. With a professional focus of a medic, he wrapped the wound tight in a clean bandage.

"That'll do you."

"Thank you," he breathed out, a little shaken. "How much do I owe you?"

"I'm not charging you for a quick cleanup." The man laughed. "Besides, I saw your curse mark. She curse you to do her bidding?"

He hesitated, then shook his head. "No."

"You do it voluntarily?"

"I'm hoping she will free me of the curse when I have done her enough deeds."

He watched him with a stern, searching look. "I'm not so sure that'll work."

"It has to-" His voice was cracking again. "If it doesn't, then I have nothing else."

"That's not true." The man said gently. Before Kai could respond, he pulled back his sleeve, revealing a faded, almost burned looking mark.

Kai's eyes widened. "Your curse was broken?"

"Yep. Didn't need the stone lady's help either."

"But how?"

"Some curses, are only curses because you won't embrace them." He held his hand out. "My name's Diego."

Kai, still stunned, took his hand and shook it. "Kai."

"I hope to see you back here soon, Kai. You don't need to live your whole life making your own curse worse."

Kai nodded, turning his head down. He felt strangely nervous around Diego. "Right. I shall be on my way then."

"Safe travels."

He nodded and rushed out of the store, making a fast exit from the village.

Kai could not get Diego out of his head. Even as he scrubbed stone plates to a shine. Even as he sharpened the knives - and accidentally cut himself thoughtlessly. Even as he wiped the floor freshly clean behind the witch as she walked. Even as he brushed and cleaned her furs until not a single strand lay out of place. All this time he thought obsessively about his conversation in the village. The memory of the faded curse mark had imprinted itself into his memory, clear as his own reflection in the walls where he polished mechanically.

He stared at his own face, suddenly seeing in a fresh light - the way Diego must had seen him. He looked tired, a bit sickly, hair lank and dirty, and his skin was way worse than it had ever been. He'd hardly been the image of perfection before, but now he could see how the witch had taken her toll on him - either through her errands or the curse itself.

He wondered if his appearance put her off him.

Cutting his own hair was harder than he expected, especially with the stone knives instead of scissors. With limited water, he couldn't even wash it properly, so the only way to neaten it was to make it too short to notice. In the end it turned into a mess, stuck out at weird angles, and just looked worse than it had before. The witch, naturally, had sneered at him and told him to stay out of her sight until he could make it decent again.

Diego made him sit still as he attempted to fix it with a pair of medical scissors. "You're lucky you didn't cut yourself."

"I'm not clumsy." Kai responded, blinking rapidly as stray hair fell into his eyes, "I'm just not… Skilled."

"Sure. Are you still running all those errands for the witch?"

"Yes."

"This had better not be for her too."

Kai chewed his tongue.

Diego stopped cutting. Setting the scissors aside he gently set his hands on Kai's shoulders, fingers giving a light squeeze. "Why are you doing this, Kai?"

He kept his gaze down. "Maybe if I looked less… Pathetic… She might take me more seriously."

"Kai, you could look like royalty and she wouldn't treat you any better. She wants you to look pathetic."

"So I never should have cut my hair…"

"So you should get out of there. You don't owe her your services."

Kai turned to him quickly, eyes wide and panicked. "But my curse!"

"Will not be changed by her any time soon, not if she can keep using you." Diego spoke gently, though his tone was firm. "You need to get out of there."

Kai clenched his jaw. "And go where? I am cursed. I cannot return home."

"Anywhere is better."

This calm attitude felt like a knife. "Perhaps for you. Fortune clearly takes favour for some." His voice was more bitter than he expected, and he stood. "I'm sorry to have bothered you. Evidently my company brings you distress, as it does to all."

"Kai-"

"Your payment." He stiffly forced the coins into Diego's hand before making a swift exit. He kept his head low to hide the way he chewed his lip, bitter hurt bundling in his throat.

"You look like a child," the witch commented dryly when he brought her food. "Though it's slightly better on the eyes than before."

He nodded, sucking his cheeks between his teeth and biting down.

"Who cut it? I know you didn't."

"Someone in the village."

She huffed a dry laugh, scornful. "Do they take such pity on you? I'm surprised they didn't shave a line down your head and parade you around the shops to laugh at."

Kai bit his cheeks harder. He was beginning to regret his earlier attitude to Diego. "They can show great kindness sometimes."

"They're making fun of you. None of them want to waste their efforts being friends with a cursed little mouse like you. No doubt they will gossip about you around the village, and they'll all laugh at how miserable you are."

Kai restrained a dry sob.

Rainfall was rare a rare in the Stone Hills. But when it did come, it invaded the landscape like a pest. Kai huddled down against the large rocks, seeking what little shelter he could, as the water barrel steadily filled up. Carrying the full container all the way back would be painful. Getting it up to the highest point of the hills had been hard enough.

No doubt the witch would immediately use everything he had gathered for a hot bath.

He nearly snapped his spine scraping and dragging it back, the skin off his hands rubbed and cut bleeding before he had even got half the distance. The rain seemed to fall heavier with every step he took, slapping his face in cold bullets. By the time he reached the grove it was torrential.

The witch had sealed the door shut. Probably to keep the rain out.

Kai stood and stared, drenched down to his shivering soul and helpless to the elements. She wouldn't hear if he knocked. She probably wouldn't check out for him either.

He leaned forward and pressed his head against the door, knowing he would have to sleep outside. The stone surface was icy and rough against his skin. Rain drizzled down it and pooled against his brow. The storm seemed louder, harsher, colder here. He closed his eyes and took a deep breath.

When he finally opened them, his gaze dragged to the barrel of water he'd gathered for the witch. He'd walked a long distance to maximise the heavy rain, but here it seemed just as wet - if not more so.

He realised with a nauseating pang that he'd been sent away deliberately.

If he slept here, or a mile away, it made no difference.

With a sudden, unexpected weight lifted off his shoulders, he turned from the door and began to walk away.

Kai curled up at the bottom of the hills and shivered. He had nowhere to go, but then it didn't make a difference. He would still be wet and cold at the door.

The rain suddenly stopped over his head, the clatter of water on stone dropped to a deep drumming on tarp. He looked up to see Diego stood over him with a large umbrella.

"This is no weather to be outside."

Kai looked down at his feet. "You don't have to pity me like some dying animal. Not after the way I behaved."

"I don't pity you, Kai. I just want you to be okay. And out here you're not going to be okay."

He scowled.

"Come on, feeling bad for yourself out here isn't going to resolve your problems any time soon." Diego held a hand out to him.

"Why do you care?" He didn't mean to sound so sharp.

"Because you're a person, Kai. And so am I. Now get up. I'm not going to carry you to salvation, but I will at least walk with you as much of the way as I can."

As all storms did, the dark clouds and rain passed and dried up. Kai's hair steadily grew out. His skin became less irritated and started to develop a healthy tone. The curse mark, though still visible to anyone who may glance at it, seemed to have faded like new skin growing over a tattoo.

"How are you feeling?" Diego asked, gently trimming Kai's hair into a neater shape.

"Better. Still kinda bad."

"Sometimes getting over something can be just as painful as the thing itself."

Kai tilted his head back to look at the other. "How did you get so wise?"

"People tell me their ailments and I provide them medicines. You pick up a lot from the people you meet over the years."

Kai smiled, soft if a bit tired. "So are you my medicine?"

Diego laughed and stroked his hair. "Cute, but no. Or at least I'm not the only one."

"Well... You taste the least bitter."

Diego leaned down and kissed his brow gently. "Thank you. I appreciate it."

A Long Time Ahead

Things didn't talk in the desert wastes. From what I'd observed, nothing really moved out here either. Only wind twirled its way through the remnants of the old town, its buildings now reduced to posts and foundations. At night they looked like fingers poking through the earth.

Some life had survived. Little sand creatures, some flat and smooth as the planes and others rounded and rough like stones, hid in the tiny crevices of sand-worn bricks. Some sailed on low wings across flat, dusty surfaces like moving floors, and others dragged their heavy bodies slowly across the landscape, leaving wide tracks in their wake.

The worst of them flew high above, circling the sun and casting huge shadows over their prey. I always kept my distance from them. Just one of the beasts could tear an arm off. They, at least, were not common around these parts. Most living things weren't.

Despite all this, I liked it out here. Quiet. One colour. Always easy to tell what was and wasn't real. In the wind the sand may whisper, but it never says anything. Things that creep or seep or stretch in the shadows don't belong out here. It's safe.

I know I have always seen the way shadows turn to watch me as I walk by, heard them talking in quiet rooms and the strange whispers in my ear at night. As a child I thought this was what thinking was. I thought this was imagination. I thought very wrong, of course.

I knew things weren't as they should be when one of the shadows peeled away from a wall and joined me on my walk home, silently floating just at the corner of my eye. By the time I reached my doorway, it had vanished. I waited a moment before going inside, finding my family sat together in the front room. A quick enquiry revealed that they hadn't seen anyone walk past the window other than myself. In fact, they'd never seen anyone hang around our neighborhood at night.

I kept my mouth shut from then on.

My home town was not a busy place, but the voices of others was often a possibility, and during the evenings before it became too dark many people were making their own way home. It became increasingly difficult to know if I was being spoken to or not.

So I packed and left.

Out in the empty brown sands, away from civilisation, I was safe.

I had been alone for a long time before that day I noticed the shadows in the distance. The massive creatures soaring through the sky had gathered short distance away, orbiting the orange sun. They moved faster than usual, descending steadily, huge leathery wings and spined tails causing the sand beneath to stir and twist up and create a small sandstorm. The brown haze beneath them became denser and denser as they spiraled lower on whatever poor creature had pissed them off.

I watched the from behind a strange, crumbling wall where I had found shelter against the gritty breeze, my belongings tucked neatly against its slanted base. With any luck I'd be able to stay there overnight. With even more luck, I'd avoid any beast confrontations. I turned away from the fray and kept my head down, focusing on making sure I still had plenty of food and water to keep me going until I next had to hunt.

I was in the process of decompressing some food to eat that night when some unusual noises caught my attention: loud voices shouting. Voices that called indistinct words, alarmed and chaotic. Though I couldn't make out what they were saying, there was an obvious tone of alarm. It was starkly different to the quiet mumbling voices I had become accustomed to. I leaned over the wall and peered down, squinting through the dust clouds to spot three travelers. They were all cloaked against the sun with large bags, on foot and running. The flying creatures had obviously chosen them as prey, and were swooping down on them in sharp arcs, herding them close together. The travelers looked completely unarmed, and definitely unprepared for what lived out here.

They wouldn't survive.

I hunched back down behind the wall. I shouldn't interfere. It was incredibly dangerous. Chances were the beasts would only take one of them and leave the other two lightly maimed. They would be fine.

They screams got a little louder.

I drummed my hands on my bag, chewing my lip. A little sweat had started to build on my neck, tickling the short hair I'd cut back with a knife. Keeping to your own out here was the way to stay alive. Keeping to myself out here was how I kept myself going. Engaging with people only made things worse.

And yet.

It was a cruel thing to let people die. It would be inhumane to just allow those so vulnerable to be torn to pieces just because it might make me uncomfortable for a short while. I couldn't just be a hidden bystander, especially when the pack of flying beasts got steadily larger, crying out their strange, warbling war song.

I groaned and rummaged through my bag, searching until my fingers locked around a small wooden object. I yanked it out, untangling the attached string from the other contents. The wind whistle never looked impressive, all flat and made dark with hardening polish, but anyone intending to travel would rest their livelihoods on it. I gave the attached string a few harsh tugs, checking that the old, waxed knot was still holding up. All good to go.

I took a deep breath and snuffled around the wall, eyeing the beasts with the whistle in hand. I let the string slide through my fingers until the whistle was hanging down a few feet, then began to twirl it in slow circles to get it started. It made an uneven wail until I start letting out more string, spinning it in faster and wider circles. The slow wobbly tone drew the attention of several of the flyers who steered around towards me, not yet aware of what was to come.

With a twitch of my wrist the spinning sped up and I lifted the whistle above my head, letting it swing out in wider arcs above me. It immediately jumped in pitch, screaming through the sky as the flyers drew in.

They barely came close before the pitch became unbearable and they jerked back. Some twisted in the air and swooped away, heading high up out of range. Others writhed and lost the wind beneath their wings, cascading to the ground and landing heavily in huge sand clouds. The shroud of sand allowed me to move around, catching more off guard and turning them away from the travelers. The longer I spun the whistle the louder and more obnoxious it became until being even within sight of me was too much to bear for the beasts, and they turned over and swooped away.

I gave the whistle a few wider swings to encourage them off faster until it was all clear. I let the little instrument swing once more before it dropped down into my palm.

Silence returned once more over the desert as the warbling song of the flyers faded away. I gathered all the string into a loop and pocketed the whistle, keeping an eye on the travelers. They were still some distance away, trying to retrieve all their dropped belongings. They were a bit worse for wear, but safe at least.

I backed up, keeping my head down, and turned away to rush back to my wall. I didn't want to talk to them. They were fine. They could continue on their journey and I could go back to my lonesome ways.

I settled myself back down and began to set up camp, unpacking my heated sleeping bag and warding pulse that kept away critters that might try to chew on me. The unexpected presence of people earlier had me a little on edge, and my fingers fumbled. I took a slow breath and counted backwards, waiting until my tremors subsided until I could turn on my food cooker without burning my fingers.

The sun set, slow and gentle down the sky. What small bumps and rocks on the ground became stretched black cracks across the ground. This is the hardest time of the day for me. The light makes things unclear, never certain if things are moving or not. The line between reality and my own visions became blurry. So, when long shadows drew nearer to me in the darkness, I paid no mind to the ones approaching.

"Hey, there!"

I jolted and shrunk back, head jerking up to meet the shiny eyes of the figures. Apparitions never spoke with such clarity.

"We're from before. You helped us out."

I squinted, taking in the layered cloaks and hoods, the pattern of distant tribes woven into the heavy fabric. The image of them running together with the fabric raised over their heads resurfaced in my memory. I nodded, once, too startled to attempt to form words.

"We have some spare food if you'd like to share? We owe you."

I took my time considering it, dropping my gaze to my hands. I travelled alone for good reason, but turning down free food in the wastes was the sort of stupidity that could kill you a week or two down the road.

"We won't bother you if you don't want us."

I glanced up at the sincere expressions. It was probably rude, at this point, to not give any response. I nodded, quick and awkward, and shifted back, gesturing my hand to the space in front of me in what I hoped was an inviting way.

They smiled and settled down opposite me, taking out bags from beneath their robes and unpacking dried foods. Some were cooked in the way I was used to, attached to thin sticks to hold them together on the cooker. Others were placed in a metal case set up on top of it, probably to preserve the moisture. You needed any kind of hydration you could get out in the dry, barren landscape.

They talked. A lot. Mostly among themselves, but also to me about their journey. They had been travelling for months by the sound of it, seeking an old underground sewer system they believed housed a long lost branch of their tribe along with forgotten ancient customs they hoped to restore. It seemed like a nice, if dangerous, idea. I just nodded along in response, which they seemed perfectly content with.

"We just need to find signs," one of them, the shortest, explained. "Something that might look like the remains of the sewers or an access point."

I bit into a roasted vegetable, breathing in as I chewed to experience as much of the rich taste as I could, savouring the rare delicacy. I knew they'd have a hard time finding anything like what they were after out in the middle of nowhere. There weren't any potholes in the sand, and any structures had worn away long ago, let alone any resembling huge pipes. I didn't say anything, though my expression must have given away my doubts.

"I can almost hear your thoughts. But believe us, we've done a lot of research," another, the tallest, insisted.

I nodded in a neutral, non-responsive way and drank my water.

"All we need to find is some sort of sign. Any kind of structure with a rounded surface."

I kept drinking, eyes down, without bothering to respond. After a minute, I became suddenly aware of them all staring at me. I swallowed and shrunk back, shy under the attention. My back settled into the rounded stone of the dip we were in.

I realised then that they weren't looking at me, but behind me. After an awkward pause I turned, laying my eyes on the large, curved wall. As though to confirm its shape, I raised a hand and patted the dusty layer of sand settled in the cracks. Clumps fell away, some more stubborn needing a dig and tug, and slowly revealed the lines and corners of filler between brick.

"That's sewer wall if I ever saw one!"

I pulled my hand away and wiped it on my shirt.

"We must be closer than we thought, this is great news!" Inspired by the discovery, the group began to plan out their next part of the journey, to follow where they believed the pipe lead.

They were very loud now.

I'd kept my peace, afraid of replying to someone who wasn't there, or to words that hadn't been spoken, but now I knew I had to step up. You can't be making a racket at night, no matter how many pulses you set up.

I raised my hands and made pressing gestures, shushing as loudly as I could without feeling like I was contributing to the noise.

But it was already too late. Even I could identify the dangerous reality of the dark shadows that had risen into the sky and begun to circle the moon.

They finally fell silent, all eyes turned to the flying beasts, now more terrifying than ever, blotting out the stars above. We all backed up against the sewer wall.

I knew in that moment that I couldn't hesitate anymore.

I dug the whistle out once more, gave myself a quick mental pep-talk, then stepped out into the empty sand planes.

The beasts began to descend.

I raised my arm and spun the whistle, hard and fast as I could, the high-pitched screeching cutting through the muffling silence of the night. My own ears rung with the sound.

The beasts backed away, wailing in distress.

But now the sound had turned into screams in my ears, the cries of monsters that rose from the sand. I was so very small as the largest, most monstrous beast loomed over me, closing in despite how hard I spun the whistle.

A hand squeezed my shoulder and I turned, sharp and wide-eyed.

"They're gone."

I looked back. Nothing. The world was so, so quiet. The whistle hung limp from my hand.

"Thank you. You saved us, again."

I nodded. I was shaking.

"Are you okay?"

I nodded again, quick. I swallowed and looked down.

"Do you want us to do anything for you?"

I shook my head in sharp motions, almost hurting my neck.

"Listen, it's been a pleasure meeting you, and you've done so much for us, but we must set off. We could be very close to finding the sewers!"

I nodded and met the eyes of the travelers. Of course they had to go. It was for the best. For all of us.

"Is there anything we can do for you?"

I started to shake my head, then paused. I pushed past them and crouched to rummage in my bag. Eventually I found it, then shuffled back to them, hands clutched tight around the little object.

"What is it?"

I held out a wind whistle. A spare, not quite as nice as my own, but just as functional.

"Really, you're sure?"

Instead of responding I simply pushed the whistle into the palms of the closest traveler.

"Thank you. Here, in return."

A small carved wooden pendant on a string, patterned in the way their fabrics were.

"Show this to any of our tribe and you will receive aid. It's the mark of an ally."

I accepted it carefully, containing my surprise, and tied it secure around my wrist. Before I probably would have stuffed it at the bottom of my bag. Now I wanted it there, close, safe. A reminder. A smile pulled my lips.

We shook hands, theirs squeezing mine in a friendly, reassuring way.

Then they left, leaving me alone once more.

I settled down by my cooker, returning to the last of the food, and gazed up at the stars.

Despite My Own

The gears of the world cranked in steady, slow circles deep beneath the Earth's crust where no sun reached. Dust and clumps would occasionally fall down from the darkness into the endless depths, exploding on jutting-out slate levels where the under-dwellers shyed back in caution. None ever saw the world above, too far down in the bottomless pits to try.

In the rumbling quiet, deep below, a lone dweller sat on her slate level. She took a stone from the ground, fallen from above, and turned it over in her palm. Her heavy chains scraped on the ground, but it had long since stopped bothering her. She swiped mud and dust from the stone to find its surface smooth, shiny and coloured. It glinted in the foreign way of things that didn't belong.

Rarer than anything she'd seen fall before.

Her fingers rubbed and smeared the dust and earth off until it was slowly polished as clean as she could, clutching it tight to her palm. Carefully, so as not to drop it, she turned the stone around between her fingers, watching the way even the very dim light danced on its edges. It seemed to have been cut into a specific shape rather than just ripped from the ground in a natural formation, and had a hole running through it - likely so it could hang off something.

But what? Where had it come from?

She raised her head to stare up into the darkness above. Somewhere up in the cavernous expanse something distant caught the light for a split second. She squinted, trying to make out whatever it was. With a sudden 'whoosh' sound, the object plummeted past her face and hit the ground with a hard bounce, leaving a wet splatter on the floor and flicking droplets up into the air. She flinched in alarm, holding still to see if anything would happen, then steadily inched closer. She extended a hand out, brushing fingertips to the dirty wet ground, then recoiled upon finding it warm. Her fingertips were stained dark.

Blood.

The fallen object gleamed, large and shiny and coated in wet blood. Wherever it had fallen from, something - or someone - was hurt. Possibly fatally.

But they had got up there in the first place.

She tucked the round objects, which she suspected may be grand beads, into the folds of her raggedy clothing. With a great effort she staggered towards the walls, stunted legs barely shakily supporting her weight. She didn't worry about them normally, choosing to stay where she was without disturbing the chains, but now she needed to start moving if she hoped to get to whoever was up there. She gripped a jutting rock with her roughed hands and took a heavy breath before hoisting herself up, wrists burning with pain where the shackles clenched to the bone. She grit her teeth, eyes pricking with tears, and worked her way up slowly, crawling shaky and beetle-like to the next platform.

She collapsed onto the slate, heaving and shaking. Bile burned her tongue and she swallowed it back. She lay there for a moment, waiting for the pain to dull to a manageable ache, before picking herself back up. She was used to this, having had to do it on occasion to scavenge for food. The real struggle wouldn't happen until further up. She took a deep breath, then began the climb again.

It was an excruciatingly long, exhausting process. Each climb became harder and slower than the last. Her wrists were red and swollen, flesh pressing against shackle, and the chain heavier than ever. It took hours for her to reach the top platform, wheezing and sweating, body trembling with pain. She lay for some time on the edge, vision swaying in and out.

Eventually the ache subsided enough to bare and her breathing settled down. The slate beneath her was wet and sticky with her sweat, her body peeling from it as she pushed herself up. She wiped her raw, leaking eyes, puffy and red from crying, and turned her head up once more.

Far above the gears continued to turn, their deep grinding sound slow and echoing. Her eyes narrowed as she tried to focus on the shapes. One of the smaller gears didn't seem to be turning properly, out of tune with the rest. It jerked and stopped, rotating back before jerking again, its nearby gear clunking awkwardly against it. Something had become lodged in the gargantuan metal contraption. As she stared up at it, trying to identify what was going on, another sparkling stone plummeted down and hit the floor at her feet. It made a huge, wet splat and covered her toes in warm blood as it bounced away.

Sickness tugged at her gut.

She couldn't imagine why anyone would go up there, nor how they had been caught. No one ever went up to the world gears. There was nothing up there except danger and death.

Despite this, there was a way up. For maintenance, she assumed. It was a long, long climb up steep steps and shaky ladders. No one in their right mind would bother going up without damn good reason.

Her feet slipped precariously over the edge several times as she made her steady ascent. The steps were uncomfortably narrow. She struggled to keep her legs stable enough without tripping down. Often she found herself hunched on all fours, strained wrists keeping her from falling.

By the time she was high enough to see what was blocking the cog, the distant pained groans had echoed down to her ears. Whoever was stuck up there, they were still alive. If only barely.

It was just enough to motivate her final steps up to the first gear, the great metal piece turning slow enough for her to climb onto and catch her breath. Like a strange tree animal she slowly crawled across the time-roughed curved metal, approaching the hanging bridge leading between each part. It wobbled as she pulled her tired weight onto it.

She managed, inch by inch, to shuffle herself to the other side. The frame creaked beneath her and swayed, but she continued as best as she could. When she reached firm flooring once again she gripped it with her palms, wheezing. It was drenched in blood. Raising her head she could just make out the dark shape of a person wedged between two cogs. A thick drop of blood fell and hit her face. She didn't bother to wipe it, swallowing hard before she dragged herself to the little flight of steps at the end of the level.

It took far longer than she wanted for her to reach the trapped person. At a guess he looked to be a young man with tidy dark hair that had been wrecked by distress, draped in flamboyant garments hiked around his legs where they'd become wedged. Blood oozed from between the cogs, soaking his clothes and skin. It wasn't a pretty sight.

She leaned closer, extending an arm to gently nudge whoever this stranger was. Unconscious. It made sense, given how long she had taken to get up here - the immense pain and blood loss would knock anyone out. This wouldn't deter her, though, and she quickly improvised by using the sharp edge of her shackles to cut at the fabrics until they fell loose. With each clump of sticky material she yanked the person closer to her and away from the cog, flinching whenever it shifted.

The process of freeing him seemed to take longer than her journey up. She'd take a deep breath, quickly yank on his shoulders until he couldn't move anymore, then reach out to hack at the fabric. She silently called out to any greater power, begging that nothing would go wrong. Once the cog jerked so unexpectedly that she'd cringed, holding as still as possible until it was safe to move again. After that she'd moved even slower than ever. It took a long, long time until the young man was free.

He fell to the ground like a dead weight, torso making a wet thud on the solid platform. For a sickening moment she thought it was too late. Panic shocked through her and shook her bones. Then with a stroke of relief she saw his chest was still rising and falling, if barely.

She was very used to blood by now, even if the quantity of it was a little discomforting. It was a fairly simple task to stem the flow from the worst of the damage, especially as she had all this cut off fabric to use. She barely noticed the pain in her wrists while she bandaged the wounds, wiping the clots away the best she could. Nothing had dried to scabs, but it had congealed and stuck to his flesh. Now and then she had to saw away bits of fabric that were just too ruined by blood or fraying to use, and each minute lost felt like a death sentence to this poor man.

Eventually she had done all she could do for him. She sat there with his head on her knees for some time and waited.

And waited.

Waited…

Finally, the man's eyes fluttered and her heart nearly gave out with relief.

He murmured something, voice weak and rough from screaming in pain. She leaned a little closer to listen and he murmured something else. She realised he was speaking in a language she didn't know. She blinked down at him helplessly.

He frowned and shifted to try to sit up, then winced as she put a hand on his shoulder. Starting to notice that something was wrong, he looked down.

There was a scuffle where he shouted and panicked and she had to calm him, carefully pushing him to hold still so he didn't cause excessive bleeding. Then he panicked more when he saw her shackles, horrified by the state of her arms and hands. It took a significant amount of gentle hushing and backing away for him to settle down

It then took an immeasurable amount of time after to get him to a point where he was remotely able to comprehend his situation. Based on his clothes and gestures as he spoke, she reasoned that he'd come from the above and somehow, likely in some complicated accident, fallen down. Usually objects fell from the above. Not people.

It would be a challenge to get him back up there. Probably impossible. She couldn't figure out how to tell him this. To make things worse he kept gesturing upwards and repeating something insistently.

There was no way he could survive below. He had to go home. Or at least try.

This revelation posed its own problem. There was only one way up that anyone knew of, and the only people who had attempted it either fell down or were never heard of again.

There was no way about it. They'd have to climb the cogs themselves.

This was hard to explain, and involved a lot of pointing and miming. Once she had managed to get the message across, it was even harder to convince him that it was the only way. There was a lot of head shaking and frantic words. She insisted, giving him an apologetic look - she was hardly thrilled about it either.

He took it very poorly. Moping on the floor. Wailing. Gesturing at his ruined legs. It was the most resistant she had ever seen anyone be about anything.

She waited through it all patiently. It was more than reasonable for him to be this upset. She'd been much the same when she'd had the metal shoved into her arms permanently. Possibly more dramatic, and definitely sulked for longer than he had. Even now she felt the exhausting emotional weight of her own displeasure. He was taking this very well in comparison.

But unlike her, he had to get over it soon if he wanted out.

It was only after he'd gone through a stage of talking to himself and looking into the darkness that he eventually relented. But with one stern motion of his hand and a few punctuated words, it was very clear what their main issue was: moving him. His legs were far too broken to stand, with or without help. Climbing up would not be an easily possibility.

With no other option, she accepted her fate.

Each of the massive gears had large protective tubes around their bases, wide and solid enough to support the heavy metals, preventing rust or cracking or whatever else may threaten the great under-earth machine. They were definitely rough enough to grip with bare hands, and wide enough to sit on. Thankfully they held still while the massive cogwheel turned.

With all the effort she could muster, she pushed him, legs and arms shaking, up to the first gear. His hands brushed against the edge, pawed at the surface, didn't catch at all, and they both toppled over onto the hard floor. They both lay for some time staring up in the darkness, aching all over and wondering if it was even worth it.

Despite painful failure, they tried again. This time they hooped some of his finery on one of the teeth of the gears and let it slowly pull them both up. The fabric strained under their combined weight until they reached the massive beam, scraping their nails on the surface. With a considerable effort they both draped themselves onto the massive curved surface and lay panting.

They waited there for a while, regaining their energy. He pressed a hand to his wounds while she waited for the pain in her arms to subside. Their breaths had long settled when they finally sat up again. Then they tried it again on the next gear.

The first three gears took them higher than they had expected, and though it involved mostly resting and regaining strength, they just about managed it without too much trouble. Both of them were honestly impressed they'd got that far, though neither could communicate that fact to the other. Not that they had the effort to - their energies were entirely reserved for climbing.

Their upward journey reached an unexpected complication. The last gear was slightly off from the up-up-up path. In comparison to them, it was much further over than previous ones, even though on the grand scale it wasn't much. For the two injured companions it would be beyond difficult to get to.

The man shook his head, exhausted, and leaned against the nearest flat surface. His face was pale and blood seeped through the bandages. His eyes closed slowly and he mumbled something incoherent. She knew it was worthless to push him now. He wouldn't make it.

Instead she lay the fabric, now stretched taut, down and guided him to lie on it. He watched her quietly as he lay, face lined and eyes searching hers.

After a moment he shifted aside and gently pulled on her rags. She watched him, confused for a moment, until she realised he was pulling her close. Going along with his gestures, she shuffled down to lie beside him. They settled, both bloodied and aching from their wounds, and slept.

They awoke slowly, groggy, and hungry. There was no food up in the gears. Just the deep grinding. While she was used to this, her companion was obviously not. His mood was dipped, but they were both comforted to note that the wounds had stopped bleeding.

It took several tosses, punctuated by heavy sighs, to eventually hook the fabric over the far-off gear. They only had one chance once it caught, knowing if they slipped it would be fatal. They clung tight to each other, the other end of fabric wrapped around their waists. In sync they took a deep breath and hoped with all their might.

They swung across.

For a moment the two were suspended in the air, solid footing either side of them and nothing beneath. The gear hadn't yet turned enough for them to make a landing. For a gut-lurching moment she thought they would fall and die.

Then the gear teeth pulled them up just in time and they smacked into the solid metal tube, both of them winded for a second before they scrambled for purchase. They heaved themselves over by the fingertips, sweating and panting with effort, until they were both secure. They both collapsed and waited for their hearts to settle. Overhead the fabric was pulled away and chewed up by the giant metal teeth. They were fortunate to have made it to the top of the great machine.

Exhausted, she stared up into the darkness. It stared back at her. She blinked. A dim light glowed down at her from what seemed to be a crack that ran through the dark nothingness. The light was soft, round and silvery. She felt herself mesmerised by it.

Beside her, her new companion began to laugh, breathy and frantic and relieved. He waved a hand weakly at it, blabbering something she couldn't understand. Somehow, she didn't need to. She knew what he meant. She knew what she was seeing.

The above.

They were very close. Closer than she could ever have dreamed. Getting him home actually looked like a real possibility now. With her heart brimming with hope, she sat up slowly and looked around, wondering how to proceed.

There was something a short way off. A ledge poked out of the wall, a few steps leading up to it. A long, knotted rope hung from somewhere far above, the tasseled end brushing the ledge floor.

The way out.

They both stared at it, still physically and mentally drained, for some time.

The young man nodded resolutely, then pulled himself up enough to crawl forwards by his arms. She pushed herself to stand and followed after him. With a bit of maneuvering she carefully helped him up the steps onto the ledge. He was handling his pain a lot better now.

Getting him on the knotted rope was fairly simple. She wrapped it around him as she had with the fabric they'd used to get there to begin with. Actually making it so he could climb up was harder. His arms trembled, weak from constant straining, and she had to push him from beneath to move up. Her legs shook beneath her. It only worked for a few feet until she couldn't reach him anymore.

She would have to climb with him.

The rope creaked and swayed with their weight as she pushed him up from beneath, his legs and hips propped against her shoulders. Each pull up the rope made her wrists ache, fresh blood seeping from beneath the shackles. Her knees could barely grip on the rope and she had to rely on her arm strength. Though it was terribly slow progress, it was at least more than she had realistically expected.

After a while she could just make out the edge of the crack.

He reached out and gripped the edge, fingers breaking chunks off the soft earth for a moment before finding secure hold. She pushed him up and he pulled himself over, legs dangling for a moment before he crawled across the ground until he was completely secure. He vanished from her sight.

She smiled, relieved that she'd got him out. Her arms ached, her whole body smeared in both of their blood. She wondered how long it would take for her to get back down. She wondered if the ledge she'd made into her home was still hers, or if another under-dweller had claimed it. She wondered if she'd ever meet someone like him again.

Then he leaned over the crack and reached his arms down for her.

She stared at him.

He gestured his hands, motioning for her to hurry and get closer. She obediently raised her arms to him and he gripped her wrists beneath the shackles, pulling her up. The moment her legs left the rope she began to wobble and sway, terrified and unsteady. His grip never waivered, holding her like his life depended on it.

With a firm yank he managed to pull her high enough for her to free a hand to grab the edge. She struggled to get through the crack without her chains catching, and was pulled awkwardly up onto dewy grass and strong solid earth.

They collapsed down on the bed of green undergrowth, staring up at the open expanse of the sky.
He squeezed her shoulder as she cried.

Companion

Good morning, human. The sun is rising and I have done my morning stretches. I have filed down my claws on my post, but to be sure finished off on the table leg. The polished surface feels so nice on my paws. Now my routine is done, I want some breakfast - the wet food, please not the kibble. I know you are still sleeping, human, but I am hungry. Get up!

Human, you are better at this patience game than I. Because you would not move I even chose to nap with you. I was generous and put all of my body onto your chest, sharing all the warmth I have. But now the sun is up and you must be up too - I am very hungry!

Oh human, you move so slow these days - but you cannot be so old? When you call to me your voice sounds so low, so tired. I'm sorry I do not have thumbs like you, human. Let me press my head to your hands, let me thank you for your care. I will purr my loudest, my best, so you can hear me no matter where you go.

Human, you forgot to eat again. I hope you are hunting when you go out. Many plates and cups are left in the kitchen with food still on them. I've tried to lick them clean, but I threw up on the carpet. Instead I have tried to hunt down all the flies in the house, but I can't feed those to you. Please eat, human.

Human, you are so warm. I miss you when you are gone. I hoped you had gone hunting, but I can't smell food on your breath. When did you last eat? Is it hard to hunt outside of the house? You seem so tired. I will stay on the sofa with you as long as you need, even though we have been here for hours already.

Human, I have waited for you again, but the sun is so bright in the sky and I am so, so hungry. What weighs you down so much that you can barely get up? You've slept as much as I but you still seem tired. Your voice is so weak. Your sighs are so heavy.

You don't move a lot these days, human. We never play. You come home and go back to bed. I tried to bring you my toys but you ignore them. Are you sick? I can't smell it on you. Even when I nuzzle you, you just pull me to lie down. That's fine. I'll stay with you, always, and keep you warm and purr for you until you feel better.

You haven't washed in a while. I tried to groom you, but you pushed me away.

My litter tray is full. Didn't you notice at all? You haven't scolded me for kicking the litter all over the floor, either. It must smell bad to you, but you haven't done anything. You haven't moved all day. Don't you need to go out like usual? I'll stay with you.

I'm hungry.

You still won't move from your bed, even when I call to you as loud as I can. But it's okay, human, you can stay where you are. I have managed to chew open the box of kibble. I can feed myself. Please focus on getting better, human. You don't have to worry about me.

I have learned how to open other things now, not just my kibble. All the boxes and plastic bags are easy to break with my teeth and claws. I think I've found your food, human. It doesn't taste good to me, but you eat strange things.

Human, I have brought you things to eat. It is easier to scavenge for you than to hunt. I opened the bread, got the bag from the box of your breakfast kibbles, I even opened all the cupboards and pulled everything out for you to find food easily. You're still in bed, but when I brought you that slice of bread you ate it. I hope you will have the strength to get your own food soon.

You're eating again, human. This is good. It's okay if you're not moving much yet, I'll keep bringing bread to you. I'm sorry I'm not bigger and can't carry more food to you. I'll try to carry the bag of your kibbles up next, but they fall out a lot. I won't leave your side for long, human. I'll always stay with you.

Why are you shouting, human? You're finally up and out of beed, and I hoped we could play. You've even found all the food I got out ready for you to eat - though some of it looks blue now. Why are you shouting at me? I have only tried to help.

I will be living behind the couch from now on, human. I do not appreciate the loudness and all your fussing over my hard work.

Human, I know you are waiting by the food bowl. You cannot tempt me so easily with wet food. I will not come out just to be shouted at again. You have cleaned away all my efforts. I am very hurt by this.

I will accept these treats and pattings as an apology. But I am still upset. Do not raise your voice again, human, or I will go behind the couch again.

I'm glad you're eating properly again. Even though you have thrown away all your food. Did that other human who came to the door with the food boxes hunt for you? I wish I could hunt that well for you too.

Promise me something, though, human? Don't get sick like that again. It's hard for me to help you all on my own.

Fishbowl

The stone sailed through the air, bounced off the sloped earth, then dived into the pond with a loud splash. Another stone sailed after it, hitting the water's surface at a spin and skipping up into the air once more, dancing across the pond for a few feet before sinking out of sight. Elena watched it with a bitter expression as she picked up another stone, pulling her knees closer to her chest.

"Now I'll never know how to do that."

Aleks, a young boy at her side, donned in the same uniform as her, gave her a soft smile. "Of course you will. You will even one day be better than me."

She tossed her second rock like a baseball, the flat side hitting the water at full force as it rocketed into the depths. "What's the point if I won't be able to show you?"

Aleks felt his smile slip a bit and raised a hand to rub her back in little circles. "Things are not so bad. You can always show me in a video."

Her nose scrunched in response and she tossed another stone, missing the pond entirely and lodging it into the mud. "I don't want to just sit around and throw stones on my own. Everyone will start making fun of me again."

"They won't," he soothed, "there will be new people next year. You can make friends again."

Elena furrowed her brow at him, a little hurt by his dismissive words. She dropped her gaze down and crossed her arms, ducking her face into the gap. Realising he'd been somewhat insensitive, he widened the circles as he rubbed her back and leaned into her apologetically. They watched something iridescent dart across the pond water, leaving tiny ripples in its wake.

"You know," he began cautiously, "sitting and being sad won't be a happy memory."

"Sorry," she mumbled against her sleeves.

"You know that is not what I mean." He gave her back a gentle pat before slowly straightening up onto his feet, careful not to slip on the muddy bank. "Let's go."

As she raised her head to ask, Aleks reached down and grabbed her by the shoulders to pull her up. She stumbled, but was steadied as he secured a firm grip on her arm and dragged her away from the pond and out through the kid's playpark. The warm sun gently cooked the tarmac beneath their feet and bounced off the metal frames of the swing-sets. It wasn't much different to earlier days when they had lounged on the hard, plastic seats with a leg either side of the chains, battling each other on app games and sharing packets of fizzy sweets. The tarmac still showed signs of damage when they'd scraped all the skin off their elbows and knees trying to do parkour.

They stepped out onto the street where the sixth form college campus faced the open park grounds. The large 'goodbye' banners hung down over the front walls, wishing the exchange students well. Before Elena could begin mourning again, Aleks dragged her down the street with his brow set in determination.

"Do you remember," he began, "when I first came here? I had no one to talk to for so many days."

She nodded, even though he probably couldn't see it.

"You were alone, so I asked you if you could take me to somewhere. And you were so shy back then, it was like you were scared of me."

She chewed her lip, a little embarrassed. Aleks was right - bring approached by the tall Bulgarian boy who she had never even spoken to had been a little alarming, not just to mention her general social anxiety of being approached anyway. But her anxiety also made it very hard for her to say 'no' to anyone. This unexpected situation had sparked their firm friendship.

"We went to that little café, do you remember?"

Elena snorted. "Mari-Anne's? That's not really a café."

"You said that then, too!" He let out a laugh, looking back at her with an infectious grin, which Elena couldn't resist returning.

Mari-Anne's was a little hot food and drink joint that had probably been hip in the sixties and never felt the need to keep up since then. Despite its outdated wallpapers and broken speakers playing constant nostalgic tunes, the staff were friendly and the food always cheap and filling. If nothing else, it was never too busy and always welcoming to shy school students who avoided the popular (and often far too busy) food chains.

Aleks bit into an overstuffed sandwich with a satisfied noise. "I remember the first time I had this," he said through a mouthful.

"You said it was too much food between not enough bread." Elena grinned, poking the ice in her lemonade with the straw.

"But now I have learned to love it! If I had not met you, I would still be eating those dry cereal bars and sitting alone in the park."

She shrugged and picked at her food. "You'd have made other friends."

He shook his head. "No. I only wanted to be your friend."

"Yeah, but you made friends with the others." She emphasised this point by gesturing at him with a well-dipped chip.

"That is because you made friends with them too."

She huffed. Since meeting him that day she had admittedly become more open to social interaction, and had begun actually talking to her classmates. She'd even managed to slowly form herself a little friendship group - though none as close to her as Aleks. No one else would hang around muddy lakes or greasy food joints with her. Besides, they got each other in ways others didn't.

"You just need to take them to a new place," Aleks replied when she voiced some of these thoughts, "Mari-Anne's is our place. You find them a new Mari-Anne's to be yours. Not all your friends have to be the same."

She had nothing to say to that, so she drank her watery lemonade in silence.

They eventually made their way out and over to the main street, passing through the first few rows of closed businesses and often empty charity shops. They stopped in the pet shop to watch the tropical fish turn around in their tiny glass tanks. Elena felt a pang of sympathy when she imagined how sad it must be when they saw their friends be taken away.

"Do you remember the film *Rumble Fish*? The one we watched in class."

Elena nodded. "Yeah, the sad one with the angry kids, right?"

Aleks nodded. "I think I am a lot like that fish."

"Doesn't he pour it into the river at the end? It's tropical, I'm pretty sure the water would have killed it."

He hummed, a little put-out. "This is true, but think about this instead. The fish has come from far away, and then lives in a small place until it is finally sent off again to another adventure. Okay, so maybe that isn't the best for it, but then that fish has many new experiences it could not have without being moved around. And it makes the boy happy, so he frees it."

"Uh, yeah but then the guy gets shot."

"Fine, yes, he does," Aleks relented, but continued, determined to make his point. "But he is happy. And he has new experiences because of the fish. And maybe if he hadn't been shot he would have gone to free other fish or animals. Maybe he would have had new adventures and experiences."

"So am I the boy?"

Aleks grinned. "You could be. But don't get shot."

She laughed. "So you're saying when you go I have to make friends with new exchange students?"

He clicked his fingers and pointed at her playfully. "You are getting it now!"

"All right, fine. You're winning, as usual."

Aleks was victoriously smug about this.

They ended up stopping by a little store selling assorted toys and gadgets, buying themselves matching fish keychains. "So we always remember to have another adventure," Aleks said brightly.

They took their keychains down to the bridge and sat with their legs hanging over the shallow river, a bag of snacks between them and both tapping at their phones as they battled on a game. The sun wandered down the sky, on its way to one final sleep before Aleks would leave.

"You'll stay in touch, yeah?" Elena asked.

Aleks paused a moment, trying to find the words, and accidentally opened himself to lose their game.

She looked up from the screen, noting his hesitation. "Won't you?"

He put his phone down on the wood and smiled at her. "I will as long as is to be natural for us."

"What's that supposed to mean?"

He tilted his head back, letting the cool sun soak into his face. "Do I need to talk every day?"

Her brow furrowed. "Well... No. I guess not. But regular enough would be nice."

"If I'm busy will you be mad?"

"No, I guess not."

He smiled and leaned over, holding his fish keychain out to bump it against hers. "Look. They haven't spoken at all and they are friends."

She snorted and gave her keychain a small swing, making it bounce against his like they were playing conkers. He retaliated and it turned into a playful, if vicious keychain fight, the cheap chains swinging wildly as the plastic fish collided against each other. It was clear that these cheap items weren't designed for rough handling and soon the clasp on Elena's fish broke.

It dropped down into the stream and began to float away.

"Oh."

"Hey, you see? It is like the rumble fish."

"And that's what you'll do? Just float out of sight?"

"Will you just stay and disappear from mine? No. We will have ways. But we must also let our eyes see other things. Would you want to stand at the bank and watch the water forever?"

She sighed quietly. "No. I wouldn't."

"Right. So you must let me go my way, whatever way."

She nodded. After a pause she glanced at him. "Okay, but we should go and grab that fish. It'll end up in the sea and it's plastic."

"Oh, right, of course!"

They jumped up and ran down the bank, catching sight of the brightly coloured keychain bobbing in the shallow water. It took both of them jumping into the stream and splashing around to rescue it, by which time the water had washed off some of the cheap paint.

They settled on the bank, wet and muddy up to the knees. Elena looked at her faded keychain, now no longer resembling the other.

"This one is already changed from its adventure."

"I don't think it's changed well."

"It is clean and ready for a new one to change it again." He lifted his own up to compare the visible differences. "Maybe mine will change too."

She looked at them, resigning herself to the situation, until a thought occurred to her. "Okay, every time we go on a new adventure we have to change our fish somehow. Then when we next meet up we can compare them."

He turned to smile at her gently. "I like that idea." He tucked his fish back in his pocket and laid back on the grassy bank. "If I don't talk to you for a while, because I will be busy at home and the time for us will be different, please do not think you are not my friend." He said suddenly.

She looked down at him with a frown. "I would never think that!"

"Yes you would." He laughed, openly but without malice. "You would worry I was ignoring you."

She chewed the inside of her cheek, knowing he was right. Instead of replying she stored her fish away safely in an inside pocket, afraid of losing it.

"But it's not that. Honestly I have not spoken to my friends at home since I came here."

It was the first time she'd heard him mention his other friends. "Don't you miss them? Don't they miss you?"

"That's the beauty of fiends, right? No matter how far or how long apart we are, we still have this love for each other."

A smile tugged the small corners of her lips. "I guess you're right, as usual."

He grinned and winked at her. "Then as long as we do not resent each other, we will always be friends."

She couldn't resist, and grinned back.

As their evening closed to its end, they tossed stones into the stream.

Printed in Great Britain
by Amazon